THE D APPOINTMENT

A RENDEZVOUS NOVEL

R.L. KENDERSON

ISBN-13: 978-1-950918-50-8

Editor: Jovana Shirley, Unforeseen Editing, www.unforeseenediting.com
Cover image:
Photographer: Wander Aguiar, Wander Book Club, www.wanderbook-
club.com
Model: SOJ
Designer: R.L. Kenderson at R.L. Cover Designs, www.
rlcoverdesigns.com

THE D APPOINTMENT

ONE
VIVIAN

I NEEDED TO GET LAID.

There. I'd said it.

It was something I had been trying to ignore, but the problem was becoming unavoidable.

I was sexually frustrated.

I threw my pen on my desk and vaulted out of my chair, so I could pace my tiny office, hoping to clear my mind. I shouldn't be occupied with thinking about rough, masculine hands exploring my body or the tight pinch when a man pushed inside me. No, my focus should be on my career.

Over the past few years, I'd been working hard at my law firm and was *this close* to making partner. At least, I hoped I was. And that was why I needed to concentrate on what was important—my client receiving a fair settlement for harassment from her previous employer.

The thing was, my body could not get on board with

my brain because I kept fantasizing about sex. The kind that would leave me wondering if I had any brain cells left. Orgasms were my stress relief, and the self-induced ones weren't doing it for me anymore.

"Ms. Stern, are you okay?" my assistant said, her body halfway through the doorway.

I hadn't even noticed she had stuck her head in. That wasn't a good sign. I prided myself on being observant.

"I'm fine," I told her.

Amanda stepped into the room. "I've been with you for over three years now, and you seem a little on edge. Is there anything I can help with?"

My assistant was very good at her job, which was saying something because I shared her with two other associates, and I didn't know what I'd do without her, but we weren't what one would call friends. There was no way I could tell her I was thinking about sex.

"I could run and get you a coffee?" Amanda offered when I didn't answer.

Not that I needed more caffeine.

"That's actually a good idea," I told her.

"Great." She smiled at my praise. "Do you want your usual?"

"No. I think, today, I'm going to go and get it myself."

"Oh," she said with raised eyebrows.

"Yeah." I pulled my purse from my bottom desk drawer. "I need a break."

As I walked past Amanda and out of my office, I heard her mutter in awe, "But you never take a break."

She was right. Normally, I didn't need one, but up until three months ago, I'd had a live-in boyfriend of six years. Until he broke up with me out of the blue, citing that we rarely saw each other and the only time we spent together was to share the occasional meal, have sex, or sleep. He wasn't wrong.

With me being a lawyer and him working in finance, we both led very busy lives, but I thought it worked well for us. I didn't demand a lot of attention from him because I didn't need it, and I got the same back. Perfect situation. But evidently, he'd wanted someone more involved in his life.

I couldn't blame him, but I also couldn't be that person for him. Especially when he'd brought up wanting children. I couldn't get pregnant and have a child. I was looking at making partner, and as arbitrary and misogynistic as the workplace was against working mothers, I couldn't change the system. I could only work within it, and I was not risking partnership by taking maternity leave.

Unfortunately, now that I was single, it also meant I wasn't getting sex regularly. And I hadn't known how badly I needed it until I wasn't getting it anymore. I had always been a sexual person, but throughout my life, I had also apparently been spoiled by having various boyfriends to cater to my needs.

I rounded the corner as I made my way to the elevator just as Preston St. James III stuck his head out of his large corner office and bellowed, "Where the hell is Schmidt?"

Preston's assistant stood up, panic on her face, and said, "Mr. St. James, Mr. Schmidt had to cancel your meeting. I was just coming to tell you."

He scowled. "Whatever for?"

Preston was one of the managing partners with his name on the door at Benowitz & St. James, and he had always been rough around the edges, but ever since his divorce, he'd been moodier than usual.

Maybe he needed to get laid too.

His assistant shrank into herself, as if she knew he wouldn't like the answer. "His wife is in labor."

Preston's jaw clenched. He wasn't the handsomest of men, but there was something very sexy about him. He had this look. I could just tell he knew how to put it down in the bedroom.

Maybe we could help each other out...

"*Fuck,*" Preston yelled and stomped back into his office, and I shook away any thoughts of sleeping with him.

Eh. I wasn't really attracted to the man, and I refused to jeopardize everything I'd worked so hard for.

Shaking my head at myself, I continued on to the elevator. It was empty when I got on, but just as the metal doors were starting to close, a hand pushed between them, and they opened once again.

"How was your date last night?"

Two women stepped on. One of them was a receptionist named Mara, and the other worked in Records.

When they saw me, the Records clerk, Gina, said, "I'll tell you later."

4

I pulled my mobile out of my purse. "Don't mind me," I told them. "I'll just be on my phone, checking emails."

Gina studied me for a moment and shrugged before turning her attention back to Mara. "It was okay."

Even though I tried to concentrate on my cell, my curiosity was too strong. I peeked at them out of the corner of my eye.

Gina smiled devilishly.

" 'It was okay'? That grin on your face tells me it was more than okay," Mara said. "You two went at it all night, and that's why you need a second coffee so early this morning."

Gina grabbed Mara's arm and bent her knees as if she were sinking. "It was *so* good. I don't even know how many times we fucked." Her eyes shot to me and back to Mara. "I mean, had sex," she said as if she had to clean her language up for me.

I pretended like I hadn't really heard them, even as I was hanging on to every word that was said.

Mara sighed. "I want that." She groaned. "It's been too long for me."

The elevator stopped at a floor, and a group of five men got on. Gina and Mara scooted back toward me as the men barely acknowledged the three of us.

The guys were talking loudly, but I still managed to hear Gina say to Mara, "You know, if you need a dick appointment, I can hook you up with some guys who *know* what they are doing."

"I am very intrigued. Are these guys sex workers?"

"No. Just guys who are good in bed. They would do it for free."

"Bless them," Mara said sarcastically.

Gina laughed. "I know. As if they wouldn't be getting something out of it."

"Well, even as curious as I am, I actually have a date on Saturday."

"Oh." Gina pushed her hip into Mara. "Good for you."

"Fingers crossed that it will be good for me."

The two women laughed, and the elevator reached the ground floor.

The men exited first, and then Gina and Mara followed.

"Lady, are you coming out?" A man with a briefcase stared at me with his hand up.

"Sorry," I said, collecting my thoughts and rushing past him. I'd been too preoccupied with what I had just heard.

Maybe a dick appointment was exactly what I needed.

TWO
VIVIAN

As the day went on, I couldn't get Gina and Mara's conversation out of my head. I had never heard of a dick appointment until today, and the more I thought of it, the more it appealed to me.

> Me: Have you ever heard of a dick appointment?

My sister, who was never far from her phone, didn't take long to respond.

> Kat: Yes. Dick appointments are the best.

> Kat: Why? Do you need one? LMAO.

> Me: I think I do.

> Kat: Oh my God, I was joking. That doesn't sound like you.

Me: Maybe you don't know everything about me.

My sister was, in many ways, my opposite. Our whole lives, our parents had ingrained in us that we needed to work hard. There was never a talk of *if* we would go to college. It was always *when*. So, after I'd graduated high school, I'd gotten my undergraduate before starting law school.

But Kat didn't care what Dad and Mom expected of us. She was five years younger than me, and when she had finished high school, she'd moved from Minnesota to Los Angeles to pursue her dream of becoming an actress. She hadn't made it far in the industry, but she'd found her calling when it came to hairstyling. She worked at an exclusive salon, where she made great money.

Was it what our parents wanted for her? No. Did she care? Also no. I used to wish I had been strong like her when I was younger and told my parents to leave me alone. But while my sister had lucked into her career and success, I had needed to work hard to find mine. I probably wouldn't be where I was if it wasn't for their insistence on studying.

But despite the fact that I was the hardworking, *follow the rules* older sibling and Kat was the free-spirited, *did whatever she wanted* younger sister, we were close. Even being halfway across the country didn't get in the way of our relationship.

Kat: I don't know about that. I know you pretty damn well.

Me: True. But the me you know the best is the one who had a steady boyfriend.

Kat: Are you missing Gordan? You didn't seem that sad when you two broke up. Is it just hitting you now?

I laughed out loud.

Me: No, I'm not sad. I don't miss him. I've barely noticed he's gone.

Except for one thing.

Kat: Ouch. That's kind of mean. You dated him for a long time. And if you don't miss him, why the D appointment message?

Me: Because I miss sex. I didn't think I liked it that much, but I don't know the last time I went three months without getting any.

Kat: You and Gordan had sex?

I scoffed at her joke.

Me: Gordan and I are both only thirty. Of course we had sex.

Kat: Sorry. It's just that you seemed more like an old married couple than hot and heavy lovers.

Me: Just because we weren't affectionate in front of everyone didn't mean we didn't do things behind closed doors.

I'd always hated PDAs—public displays of affection. It always felt like people were trying too hard to prove something. Like, we got it. He was your boyfriend, or she was your girlfriend. We didn't need to see it. Hand-holding was about all I could take. And that was in regard to other people. I didn't need anyone to hold my hand.

Kat: But you never talk about sex.

Me: I guess I feel like that stuff is private.

Kat: So, why are you bringing it up now?

Me: Because I need a second opinion on the dick appointment aspect.

Kat: I guess it depends on who it's with. Gordan?

Me: No. He's dating someone new.

Kat: Is it a friend you're going to be hooking up with? Some guy you met at a party? Who is the owner of this D you are going to have an appointment with?

Me: I don't know.

My phone rang, and I smiled.

"Hello, Kat."

"You don't know the guy you're going to have sex with? Did you pick some rando off the internet?" She gasped. "Please tell me you didn't go on Tinder. Viv, you can't go in there blind. You need someone to show you how it works. And a stranger? That's not like you."

I rolled my eyes. "When I said I didn't know, I meant, I didn't know at all who it was going to be yet. Not that I didn't know the guy."

I could hear her sigh of relief through the phone. "Damn. You scared me."

"Why?"

"Because being single is not the same as it was six years ago. And I don't want you to do something that makes you feel uncomfortable."

"Excuse me," I said. "I'm the older sister. I have much more life experience than you."

"I will give you that, but I think I've had more sexual experience."

"Hmm, just because you've had more partners than me doesn't mean you have more experience."

"Touché," Kat said with a laugh. "Maybe I don't know everything about you."

She did though. While I'd had plenty of sex in my life, I would say it had always been vanilla. My sister probably did have more experience than me in the bedroom.

"Listen, I have to get back to work, but thanks for worrying about me."

"Always. Little sisters have to worry about their big sisters just as much as the bigs worry about the littles."

"True. Talk to you later?"

"Yes. Let me know if you get your vagina massaged."

I laughed.

"And tell Mom and Dad hi from me."

"Ugh."

This time, Kat laughed.

While our parents lived in Minnesota, I saw them almost as much as my sister did. They lived several hours away, and I didn't make it there very often. Which I heard complaints about every time I did visit.

Listen, if I couldn't find the time to get laid, I definitely didn't have time to go for a weekend visit.

"Talk to you later, sis," Kat said.

"Later."

I hit End and set my phone down. Then, I turned to my computer but just stared at it.

My sister's words reverberated in my head. Even with her worries, I couldn't help but think that maybe sleeping with a stranger was exactly what I needed. No commitment, no small talk. I could just fuck him and leave.

I pushed my chair back from my desk and headed straight for our Records department.

THREE

VIVIAN

Gina was sitting at her desk when I walked into her department. She glanced up at me and back to her computer screen before doing a double take when she must have realized it was me.

I ran my eyes across the room before asking, "Do you have a minute?"

Sighing, Gina leaned back in her chair and said, "I knew I shouldn't have said anything in front of you."

This was not starting off well. In my head, I had pictured her to be as willing to help me out as she had been with Mara.

"Excuse me?"

"You're here to talk to me about what happened in the elevator, aren't you?" She shook her head. "I told myself you were going to rat me out or chastise me, but you made me think you didn't care."

I held up my hands. "I'm not going to do either of those things."

"You aren't?"

"No."

"Oh." Gina smiled. "Okay. What do you need me to pull for you then?"

I looked behind me one more time and leaned toward her. "I'm not here for work," I said in a low voice.

"Okaaaay." She drew out the word as if she thought it was strange that I was there for a personal reason, which was understandable. Gina and I had never been anything but colleagues. "Are you going to tell me why you're here then?"

I opened my mouth, but nothing came out. My idea to ask her for help had seemed reasonable as I walked over here, but the thought of saying it out loud now seemed ridiculous.

Gina picked up a stack of papers and straightened them by patting the bottom edge on her desk. "It was nice talking to you, but if you don't mind, I need to get some work done before I go home tonight."

I mentally rolled my eyes at myself. If I could negotiate deals with other lawyers and get up in front of a courtroom full of jurors and a judge, I could ask for this favor.

"I need you to hook me up with a D appointment."

Gina's jaw dropped, and she slowly lowered the papers back to her desk. "Are you for real?"

"Yes." I didn't think I had given the impression I was joking.

"But…"

"But what?" I asked testily. I couldn't wait to hear what she thought about me.

With a quick shake of her head, she said, "Nothing." Her brow furrowed. "You really want me to find a guy for you to…"

"Have sex with? Yes. Do you think you can do that for me?"

"I mean, I can…"

I sighed, getting irritated with the whole situation. It was a yes or no question. "Would it kill you to finish your sentences?" I was beginning to think I should have listened to my first instinct and gone back to my desk.

Gina pursed her lips and narrowed her eyes.

I put my hands together and pointed them at her. "Look, either you can do this for me or you can't. If you tell me no, I will figure something else out."

She cleared her throat and snatched her phone from the corner of her desk. "Oh, I can do this for you," she said, looking at her screen.

I smiled. "Wonderful. I'd like someone who's clean-cut, and I would prefer a gentleman."

Gina snorted and looked up from her phone. "I'm confused. Do you want a date, or do you want to come?"

Craning my neck, I quickly checked behind me to make sure no one had heard her comment before turning back to her. "I want to"—I cleared my throat—"come," I whispered.

"That's what I thought." Her gaze dropped to her cell

again. "Give me your phone number, so I can give you the details once I find someone."

I rattled off my digits. "You don't have anyone in mind?"

She grinned, and something about it made me take a step back. She seemed way too happy to help me all of a sudden. "Oh, I have someone in mind all right. I just need to make sure he doesn't have plans."

"Oh." This was a good thing. *Right?*

"I'll text you when I know for sure."

I nodded. "Thank you."

She smiled again with a glint in her eye. "My pleasure."

With that, I turned around and headed back to my desk.

I wasn't there for more than an hour when I got a text.

> Unknown number: It's Gina. I made an "appointment" for you at 7 tonight.

> Me: Tonight? I can't do tonight.

I was planning to stay late and get some extra work done.

> Gina: Do you want me to hook you up or not? You didn't say anything about when, and I was under the impression you wanted it sooner rather than later.

I bit my lip. She did have a point. If I met with this guy,

I would feel better tomorrow and probably get more accomplished.

Me: Yes, I want it. Give me the details.

Gina: What's to give? His name is Dom, and here's his address.

Her next text was a location on Google Maps.

I immediately clicked on it to see where I was going. It was a residential area, but it wasn't in the safest neighborhood.

Me: How well do you know this man?

Gina: Dom is a friend of mine. You'll be fine. I wouldn't send you somewhere to get hurt, especially since your text messages would lead straight back to me.

It seemed Gina understood exactly what I was asking.

Me: Thank you.

I waited for her to tell me *you're welcome*, but it seemed she was done with me, so I was on my own for the next part of this escapade.

FOUR

VIVIAN

I HESITATED AT THE END OF THE WALKWAY UP TO THE small house Gina had given me the address to.

The home was in good shape, but the landscaping left something to be desired. Not that I was there to learn gardening tips. I was there for sex.

I took a deep breath and took my first step forward.

I didn't think of myself as a prude. I didn't really care what people did in their bedrooms as long as it was consensual, but I definitely wasn't adventurous in that area, and I was feeling out of my depth.

Which meant, I had to fake it.

I squared my shoulders before knocking on the door. This Dom guy didn't need to know that I was in unfamiliar territory.

The front door swung open, and a tall blond man stood on the other side. He had a buzzed head and tattoos on his arms. I supposed some women would think he was attractive with his blue eyes and chiseled jaw. But I wasn't one of them. When I'd told Gina I liked clean-cut men, I should have suspected she would ignore me.

I should have never asked her to do me this favor.

But I was stuck, and even though I wanted to turn around and leave, that would be rude. Instead, I pulled up my professional facade I used at work and smiled politely. "Hello. I'm Vivian. Are you Dom?"

The guy eyed me up and down and leaned his head back, shouting, "Dom, some chick is here for you. Her name is..." He looked back at me and raised his brow.

"Vivian."

"Vivian," he finished as he opened the door for me to step inside, and I sighed with relief that this wasn't the guy I was there to hook up with.

"I'll be there in a sec," a deep voice called from the back.

"I'm headed out. Talk to you later," the blond guy yelled again.

"Later, Tony."

The man stepped around me and left without ever introducing himself or saying good-bye to me.

Left alone, I scanned the room and tried not to cringe. I could tell the owner was a bachelor and didn't have a lot of money. The furniture was old and mismatched, but that wasn't what bothered me. It was very messy. There were clothes thrown on the back of the couch, a pile of shoes lay in a heap by the door, a couple of crumb-filled plates sat on the coffee table along with empty beer bottles.

It wasn't exactly dirty, but it was unkempt, and again, I wondered what I was doing there.

The sound of footsteps turned my attention from the living room to the hallway, where a person who had to be Dom stepped out.

I held my breath as the dark-haired man grabbed the ends of the white towel wrapped around his neck and stared at me. A glint in his hazel eyes was followed by him licking his bottom lip, which was full and dark pink. The sexiness flowed off of him like it was a tangible thing I could touch, and I was entranced by him. I was also wet.

"You must be Vivian," he muttered.

Hearing him speak was enough to break me out of my stupor, and I swiftly became aware of the rest of him.

Besides the towel, he only had on a pair of well-worn jeans and a silver chain around his neck with a gold medallion. He had a dark beard that framed his perfect mouth, a nose piercing, an earring, and tattoos that covered not just his arms, but also his chest and his neck.

He was the exact opposite of who I would date in real life—from his home to his appearance. Gina had really missed the mark.

I held up a finger. "One moment, please." Reaching into my purse, I found my phone and pulled it out.

> Me: Gina, is this some kind of joke? I'm sure your friend is perfectly nice, but he isn't my type.

Rather than text me back, Gina called me.

"This is Vivian," I answered.

A deep sigh sounded on the other side. "You are a really hard person to do a favor for."

I winced, feeling guilty. "I apologize. It's just that—"

"Look, do you want to get off, or do you want to find a new boyfriend?"

The question was similar to the one she'd asked me earlier today.

My eyes darted to Dom, and I turned my back to him, as if that would make my conversation more private, before I answered, "The former."

"That's what I thought."

"But—"

"But nothing. Dom is going to give you the best orgasm of your life, and God knows that's exactly what you need."

"Excuse me?"

"And I know you think you're better than him, but, honey, Dom doesn't need you. He can get pussy whenever he wants. There is nothing special about yours, so if I were you, I wouldn't waste this opportunity."

My jaw dropped. I was speechless.

"Should I tell him you've changed your mind, or are you staying?"

My phone was plucked from my hand from behind me, and I spun around, coming face-to-face with Dom's chest. A fleeting thought of what he would taste like if I licked him flashed in my head.

"She's staying," he said into my phone. He hit End,

slipped my bag from my arm, put my cell inside, and set it on the floor.

"How do you know I'm staying?" I asked.

He moved forward, causing me to step back until my butt hit the wall. I swallowed hard.

Dom caged me in with his arms on either side of my head and met my eyes. "Gina said that you need to get laid. That's why you're here, are you not?"

Heat rose to my cheeks. "Yes," I admitted, but I didn't want him to forget the most important part. "But I need a little more than to just get laid."

He tilted his head to the side, not picking up on my subtle hint.

I cleared my throat. "I need to come."

He grinned. "Oh, you'll come all right." He stepped back and bit his lip as he studied me. Grabbing my hand, he pulled me toward the hall. "Let's go."

FIVE
DOMINICK

WHEN GINA HAD MESSAGED ME, ASKING IF I COULD DO
her a favor and have sex with this stuffy lawyer she worked
with, my immediate response was no.

I liked to have fun in bed, and fucking someone uptight
was not my idea of a good time. But Gina practically
begged me, and I owed her a favor for helping me out in
the past. So, I'd said yes and resigned myself to some
boring sex this evening.

Except when I saw Ms. Uptight Lawyer standing in
my living room, I changed my mind about how boring
tonight was going to be. Gina hadn't told me that Vivian
had a banging body that she covered up with her conserva-
tive clothing or that her taut brown ponytail would be
perfect for me to wrap my fist around and pull.

I wasn't sure what I had pictured in my head, but it
hadn't been this woman.

And I could tell by the look in her eyes, the feeling was mutual. The flare of desire showed in her entire body—from the small gasp she let out to the way she brushed her thighs together. The best part was, she didn't even seem to realize she had done it.

And now, I was going to have no-strings-attached sex with her. I mentally rubbed my hands together in triumph as I showed Vivian to my room. I spun around once I closed the door, but I didn't approach her just yet.

"So, you're here for some good fucking?"

Her cheeks reddened, but I held in my laugh.

"What do you like?"

Her brow furrowed. "What do you mean?"

I chuckled. "What gets you off? What makes you horny? What makes you come?"

Slowly, one shoulder went up. "I don't know. Just sex."

My eyebrows flew up as I tried not to laugh. This chick was more hard up than I'd originally thought.

"In that case, why don't we just have a little fun? You can stop me if you don't like something."

Vivian's eyes darted back and forth around my room, momentarily pausing on my bed. I wasn't that surprised. She probably had a headboard and footboard that matched the rest of her bedroom furniture. My mattress and box spring had neither of those things and sat directly on the floor. Also, my dresser didn't match either of my night-stands, but I didn't care. She probably didn't approve, but she wasn't here for the scenery.

Her gaze landed back on my face. "Okay."

Putting my hands on her hips, I guided her backward toward my dresser until her butt hit the edge.

"Why don't we start with something easy?" I knelt down, skimming my hands down the outside of her thighs.

She had on a straight, formfitting skirt that showed off her hips, but it was twice as long as what most women I brought home wore, landing just above her knees.

I lifted one of her feet and pulled off one modest heel and then did the same with the other side. I was glad to see she wasn't wearing any pantyhose, which kind of surprised me, but it would make getting into her underwear a hell of a lot easier.

I ran my hands up the backs of her legs, pausing at the hem of her skirt to see if she would stop me. She didn't utter a sound. She just watched me from under her thick lashes as she gripped the edge of the dresser while I continued toward her sweet spot.

When I got to her round ass, I slid my fingers underneath her panties and gently squeezed her cheeks. A soft moan fell from her lips.

Good sign.

Tracing one hand over her hip, I made my way to the front and in between her legs. I hadn't even parted her yet, and I could tell she was wet.

"Damn, *chica*, you are soaked."

And my erection was now hard as steel. There was nothing better than a drenched pussy, and I didn't understand why some guys didn't want their partners to be as turned on as possible.

Vivian's cheeks turned pink again, but her chin lifted as she said, "I asked for this appointment for a reason."

I snickered. "This appointment?" I repeated. As if she were coming in for an oil change or something.

"Yeah. This D appointment."

I grinned. "A dick appointment. I don't think I've ever heard someone call it that. I like it."

"What do you call it then?"

"Good ol'-fashioned fucking, baby." I pushed two fingers into her tight hole.

She parted her thighs and moaned. "Whatever works."

Her pussy was silky smooth, and I could smell her now. I no longer wanted to just fuck her. I wanted to know what she tasted like.

I pulled my hand from between her legs and shoved her skirt up. It crossed my mind to just take it off, but something about eating her out while she was still half-dressed turned me on more.

I jerked her underwear down and off each foot before tugging her knees apart.

"Oh my God," she said—and not in a good way.

My eyes swung up to her face, but I didn't even have to ask her what was wrong.

She closed her legs. "I came here straight from work."

"I figured, what with the outfit and everything."

"I mean, I haven't showered since this morning."

"So?"

She licked her lips nervously. "My ex, he would only go down on me right after I showered. He said otherwise..." She looked away. "Otherwise, the flavor was too strong."

"What a fucking pussy," I muttered. I turned my attention from her face to her cunt and kissed the top of her mound. "No offense."

I could feel her looking down on me, and I gently pushed her open to me once more.

"I'm not your ex, and I don't want to taste soap and water. I want to taste you."

"Oh my God," she said again, but this time, it came out all breathy, the way it should have in the beginning.

Shoving my face between her thighs, I circled her hole with my tongue, attempting to swallow every last drop of her. She was so wet that I had to suck, so I didn't lose any of her.

I fucking loved it.

But I couldn't eat her pussy all day. I needed to give her a little of what she had come for, so I circled her swollen clit.

Her hips bucked, and she moaned.

I drew my mouth away just enough to mutter, "Oh yeah, baby." I loved turning a woman on.

Wrapping my lips around her clit, I flicked, and sucked, and rubbed it with the flat part of my tongue, working her up into a frenzy.

Vivian's breathing quickened, and soon, I was holding her up more than she was. But as she was nearing her climax, a thought occurred to me.

I pulled back, her juices covering my face as I looked up at her. "I forgot to introduce myself. Some people call me D, others call me Dom, but my full name is Dominick. And that's the only name I want you to call out when I make you come."

SIX

VIVIAN

THE ORGASM THAT TORE THROUGH ME WAS ALMOST magical. I hadn't climaxed from oral sex in years, and I'd forgotten how good it felt.

That was, until I almost fell over because my legs could no longer hold me up.

Dom, Dominick, or whatever his name was picked me up and spread me out on his bed. A fleeting thought of concern for if he ever washed his bedding came and quickly went because I didn't want to worry about things like that when I felt so good.

"You didn't say my name."

I blinked my eyes open. "I didn't say anyone's name," I pointed out. I wasn't a loud orgasmer.

"That's a shame."

"Sorry."

He smiled down at me. "No, you're not, but you will

be." He leaned over. "But right now, it's time to get you naked."

Dominick unbuttoned my blouse with efficiency and speed and pushed the sides of my shirt apart. "Damn."

"What?"

"I wasn't expecting the lacy black bra under this outfit."

"I like to feel pretty. And it matches my underwear."

He unzipped my skirt and drew it down my legs. "I'm almost sorry I missed actually seeing you wearing the panties." He lifted his chin. "Take off the rest. I want you naked while I fuck you."

My core tightened even though I had just come, and I quickly removed my blouse and bra. Normally, when I got naked with a new lover, it took me time to let him see me unclothed. But there was something freeing about not caring if Dominick thought I was sexy enough or not.

Except the erection that sprang out of his jeans after he unzipped them led me to believe he was at least somewhat attracted to me.

I licked my lips. I should have guessed that Dominick would have a big dick—otherwise, Gina wouldn't have set me up with him—but it hadn't exactly crossed my mind until now.

There was something else that I hadn't thought of either.

"You're uncut," I said in an almost whisper.

He kicked his pants out of the way and picked up my hand to wrap it around his length.

"First time?" he asked.

I nodded.

His fist tightened around mine. "Fuck, I love that."

When he stepped away, my hand fell to the bed as he walked over to the nightstand. He pulled out a packet and ripped it open. He rolled the condom on as he walked back to me.

I spread my legs in invitation.

He jerked his head to the side. "Roll over."

"But—" I bit my tongue before I could finish my complaint.

"But what?"

Shaking my head, I said, "Nothing."

I moved onto my stomach in silent disappointment. Doggy style always felt good, but it wasn't enough to get me off. I'd thought about telling Dominick that, but I realized that he'd given me an orgasm, so technically, I'd gotten what I had come here for. I had just hoped I would be able to do it with more than oral sex.

The bed dipped between my legs as Dominick knelt on the mattress behind me, and I braced myself for him to enter me and do his thing.

"Have you ever been spanked?"

"What?" I scoffed. "N—"

SMACK!

Dominick's right hand made contact with my ass.

"*Ow*," I yelled as a sting zapped through my rear end.

"Is that a good ow or a bad ow?" he asked but brought

his other palm down on my left butt cheek with the same force.

I shook at the contact. "Holy hell. That hurt."

"It's supposed to." He rubbed the two areas he had just made sore. "Now, tell me, was it a good ow or a bad ow?"

"Bad."

"Hmm...are you sure about that?"

"Yes."

"I think you might not know your own body."

I scowled over my shoulder. "You don't know what you're—"

He pushed two fingers into me, and I bucked and moaned at his sudden invasion.

"I know this wet fucking pussy is telling me otherwise."

My muscles clenched around his digits as I rotated my hips.

"I don't like it when you lie to me," he said, yanking his hand away.

"I didn't mean to." I hadn't realized that I would like having my ass slapped.

The tip of his cock slid through my folds.

"Good. Don't do it again," he said and drove into me.

His words were hard with conviction, as if we were going to be doing this again even though we both knew this was a one-time hookup.

Dominick grabbed my hips as he thrust into me, and I lifted my butt for him. As I'd figured, it felt good, but I wasn't going to climax in this position. So, the best thing I could do was make it good for him, so he could come quickly.

But that didn't happen.

He had stamina far greater than any other guy I had slept with, and the longer he screwed me, the more turned on I got. His dick rubbed my G-spot over and over again, but it wasn't enough for me to climax, and I started to feel like I was going crazy as I tried to shut out the incredible sensations that weren't quite enough.

Just when I thought I couldn't take it anymore, Dominick grabbed on to my ponytail and pulled me onto my knees, so my back was flush against his front. A strong hand clasped my breast, and he thumbed my nipple.

"What was that *nothing* about before?" he asked, still stroking in and out of my pussy with slow, deliberate movements.

I shook my head. Or I tried to. He had a tight hold on my hair.

"When I told you to roll over, you said, 'But.' But when I asked what you were going to say and you replied, 'Nothing' "—he moved his hand to my other breast—"what was that *nothing* about?"

I bit my lip and tried to shake my head. I certainly wasn't going to say anything now.

The hand that had my hair pulled tighter until my head was on his shoulder while the other moved down my chest and over my stomach. Right before he reached my pussy, he pushed the heel of his hand above my pubic bone and used his middle finger to push down on my clit.

The combined pressure of his dick hitting my G-spot and the friction on my swollen nub was exactly what I needed to come, and I exploded so hard that the hearing left my ears and my vision went black.

I'd never had an orgasm like that.

When my senses returned, I was facedown on the comforter with Dominick over me as he rode me hard. He slammed into me one last time and grunted as his cock jerked inside me, filling the thin latex that separated us.

I was still breathing hard when Dominick rolled off me and turned me to face him. His face was more serious than I'd thought it would be for someone who'd just had an orgasm.

"If you have trouble coming a certain way, you need to tell the person you're with. You need to tell me."

My eyes widened, as he'd figured out what I had been keeping to myself.

"I—it's just—I mean—"

"It's none of those things." He hauled me into his arms and kissed me. It was hot and deep, and it felt like something he should have done before sex, not after. He drew away and looked me in the eyes. "I can't help you if you aren't real with me."

I opened my mouth to tell him that, sometimes, it wasn't worth it to speak up, but I remembered this wasn't going to happen again, so I agreed with an, "Okay," instead.

"Good. Because while I'm the first guy to make you

come like that, I shouldn't have to pull that information out of you."

My mouth fell open. "How did you know?"

"I ain't no dummy." He kissed the tip of my nose, scooted away from me, and smacked my hip. This time much gentler. "Time to go."

What?

"You got what you came for, and I have somewhere I need to be."

I smiled awkwardly. "Right." I should have been the one to get out of bed right away. I shouldn't have had to wait for him to say something.

We both stood. Me to get dressed and Dominick to go out into the hall to who knew where?

Quickly, I pulled on my clothes as fast as I could, but when I looked up, I found him leaning against the door-frame as he watched me. His arms were crossed, and he wore a look of amusement. But that was all he had on because he was still naked. Even the condom was gone.

I straightened my clothes and waited for him to move, so I could leave, but he didn't budge, so I went to squeeze past him, but he stopped me with a hand on my hip.

I met his eyes.

"Tell Gina thanks."

I frowned. "You have her phone number. Tell her yourself."

"I will. But I want to make sure you do the same."

"Oh my God. You want me to tell Gina thanks from

me, not from *you*?" I rolled my eyes. "You think highly of yourself."

"Nah. I just want to make sure Gina says yes the next time you ask her for a favor."

"I have to go." I stepped away and headed for his front door.

"Vivian."

I waited until I opened it before turning around.

"Next time, you are going to say my name."

"There's not going to be a next time," I said and scurried outside, slamming the door behind me. I rushed to my car and swiftly got in. But I did pull out my phone, and I sent a quick text before I took off for home.

> Me: You were right. He made me come. Thank you for the favor.

SEVEN
VIVIAN

By two o'clock the next afternoon, I had done more work in one day than I had done earlier in the week. In the future, I wasn't going to waste so much time before getting laid.

I was deep into doing research for a case when there was a knock on my door. I looked up to see Preston St. James standing there.

Immediately, I stood up and smoothed my skirt. "Can I help you, sir?"

I walked around my desk and attempted to peek around him to see why my assistant hadn't warned me that Mr. St. James was at my door. I could see her outside Isaac's office, which meant she was helping him. Someday, I was going to have my very own assistant.

"That was some good work you did this morning with the settlement. You got the company to agree to more than the client had originally asked for."

This was unexpected. I knew I had wrapped up the case more quickly than anticipated, saving us from spending weeks in a courtroom, but in the scheme of things, it was a small case with minimal payout. But if a name partner—a firm partner whose name was literally in the official name of the law firm—was taking notice of my work, I wasn't going to put down my accomplishments.

"Thank you. I came across some information in my research that helped them see things our client's way." Information that I had just found that morning, thanks to being able to focus after last night's activities.

"Since your schedule has cleared up a bit, I have an assignment for you."

Maintaining my composure, I made sure not to seem too excited, but if Mr. St. James was coming to me for something specific, it must mean I was doing something right.

"I would love to help. What do you need me to do?"

"Do you know the mayor?"

My eyes widened. The mayor of Minneapolis, Nadine Evans, was a beautiful woman in her early forties, who was one of the few female mayors the city had ever nominated. She'd gone to Harvard Law and returned to Minnesota once she graduated. She had been married to her husband, Corey Evans, for fifteen years, and they had two children together. I liked her views on things, and if I'd lived in Minneapolis instead of a close suburb, I would have voted for her.

"Not personally," I answered. "But I know *of* her."

"The mayor wants to put together a Women in Law program that goes around to schools in the metro area to talk to young girls about what it's like to be a lawyer."

I swallowed hard. "And you want me to be a part of this?"

"Yes."

But I didn't want to. I didn't care for children that much. I was perfectly fine with never having one of my own. And now, I had to willingly spend time away from my career to go to schools and talk to them.

Mr. St. James must have sensed my hesitation because he added, "It will look good to the board at our next meeting about partnerships." He smiled. "Besides, if I didn't think you could handle this in addition to your work-load, I wouldn't have asked you."

Somehow, I doubted that since the second thing he'd mentioned when he walked in was that I had finished my case early.

"When does this start?"

The name partner actually had the smarts to look sheepish. "This afternoon."

"This afternoon?" Is he nuts?

No, he was pressed for time, and that was why he had picked me. So much for actually being noticed for the work I did.

"Yes, and I apologize. Things have been...hectic at home, and I was only reminded of this when the mayor emailed me this morning."

I gritted my teeth. I had heard through office gossip

that Mr. St. James had gotten a divorce and shared joint custody of his son, Paxton, with his ex-wife. His mother had moved in to help with Paxton, but she had left with her new boyfriend to Cabo or somewhere like that.

His mom had come from money and married Preston St. James Jr. right out of college, ensuring she never had to work a day in her life. Apparently, caring for a toddler was too much for her.

I was surprised Mr. St. James hadn't simply hired a nanny, like his parents had done for him and his siblings, but it was none of my business. And again, most of it was hearsay and office gossip. I had no idea how much of it was true.

And now, I was going to have to suffer the consequences of Mr. St. James's personal life because we both knew I wasn't going to say no.

"Okay, give me the details, and I will be there."

Mr. St. James smiled at me, and I was struck by how handsome he looked. For a moment, I had no doubts about why his ex-wife had fallen for him.

As I made my way up to the mayor's office at City Hall, I tried to convince myself this wasn't the worst thing in the world.

Mr. St. James had forwarded me all the information, and to my relief, this was only going to be a temporary thing. The mayor was working on bringing female-identified lawyers in to talk to students for the current school year. If it went well, she was going to bring in fresh faces the next year.

Thank God because I wasn't going to waste time doing this for the rest of my career when I could actually be spending time in a courtroom or sitting across a conference table instead of convincing children to go to law school and to flood the market even more than it already was.

When I entered the suite where the mayor kept her office, I was directed to a conference room, where another woman was sitting.

As I walked in, she put her phone down and smiled at me. "Are you here for the Women in Law thing too?" she asked.

"Yes. I'm Vivian Stern," I said, holding out my arm.

"Rayne Thompson." She stood and shook my hand.

As I pulled out a chair and sat, I said, "You look familiar."

"I work for the DA's office." She smiled, but it was one of those polite ones that didn't reach the eyes. "I'm one of the newer prosecutors there, so I was the *lucky* one to be picked for this assignment."

I nodded in understanding. "I, too, was the lucky one. My boss knows I'm looking to make partner and told me this would look good on my résumé at the next partnership board meeting. I think we might have sat across from each other in court."

"So, you're in private practice?" she asked. "What's your specialty?"

"My passion is defense work, but right now, I do what is assigned to me. This morning, I finished up an employment case. My firm is big, and we take all kinds of cases from immigration to divorce to defense."

When I had graduated from law school, I had worked for the public defender's office because I wanted to help people in trouble, but I'd soon learned why most didn't stay. Public defenders were underpaid and overworked. I had hoped to fare better in the private sector, but people didn't want to pay a lot of money for someone without much of a rapport.

"Ah," she said in understanding.

"It can be a lot." I looked around the room. "And this doesn't help."

Rayne pretended to pick up a glass and raised her hand to me. "Here's to suffering through this together."

I chuckled and faked hitting a glass against hers. "Here's to suffering together," I agreed. And due to her choice of words, I opened my mouth and asked, "So, do you hate kids too?"

Rayne's eyes snapped wide. "You hate kids?"

I winced inwardly. This was why I was never good at making friends. I said too many things that were on my mind without thinking first. And unfortunately, this time, it was to someone I'd thought would make the experience a little more tolerable.

I cleared my throat. "Well, I don't hate them. Not really. I just don't get along with them. And I've never wanted my own. Truthfully, I don't know how to act around them."

Rayne's expression went from less horrified to understanding. "Do you have any siblings?"

I smiled. "Ironically, a younger sister, but only by five years, but I never had to take care of her or babysit. You?"

"I have an older brother, but I used to babysit for all the kids in the neighborhood when I was younger. Don't worry. I'll help you out with the kid stuff."

"Thank you."

Voices could be heard in the hall, and while Rayne and I turned toward the closed door, we couldn't make out what was being said.

"I heard there were going to be three of us," she said. "And if you work for a law firm and I work for the DA's office, who do you think the third person is going to be?"

"Gosh. I don't know. I wasn't told a lot before I came down here."

"Me neither."

"But if I had to guess, maybe a judge?"

Rayne snapped her fingers. "Ooh, a judge. Who else to motivate young women into the field of law than a judge?"

"You really think so? Would a judge have time?"

Rayne shrugged. "Do we?"

I laughed. "Good point."

"Besides, corporate law would make everyone fall asleep."

"But an entertainment lawyer would be pretty cool. Especially if they brought a client in with them."

"Unfortunately, we live in Minnesota instead of LA, so well-known clients are few and far between."

"Good point. It's probably a judge."

Rayne leaned toward me and smiled. "Who do you think it is? We don't have that many female judges."

"I don't care as long as it's not Judge—" I cut myself off before I could complete my thought.

Rayne seemed nice, but she could also use what I told her against me.

"Burke," she finished for me, and I laughed.

"Oh, thank God. I didn't want to say it out loud."

"She's just..."

Putting my hand up, I smiled and said, "I get it."

Judge Burke was hard to get along with, and I had yet to meet anyone who liked her. In simple terms, she was mean.

The door opened, and Rayne and I swung our heads around to see the mayor enter the room.

"Oh good, the two of you are here," she said with a grin. She turned back to the open door. "Delaney, in here." Looking back at us, she said, "The third member of this little project of mine will be here in just a second, and then I'll explain what it's all about. How does that sound?"

"Good," I said, and Rayne nodded.

"I'm here. I'm here," a cheerful voice said from the other side of the doorway, and relief went through me. I didn't recognize the voice, but I knew the voice wasn't Judge Burke.

But my smile slipped off my face when I saw who walked in.

Judge St. James. This person was probably the second-worst judge to be picked for me to work with.

After all, she was my superior, Preston St. James's, ex-wife.

EIGHT
DOMINICK

WHEN I GOT HOME FROM WORK, I FOUND MY BROTHER sitting at my kitchen table, staring at a textbook.

"Hey," I said. "When did you get here?"

"About an hour ago. I went home, but I had to leave," Spencer said without looking up.

"Ah." I knew what he meant. Either our mother was having sex or was getting high. Or both. "Let me get cleaned up, and then I'll make us some dinner."

Spencer smiled up at me. "Thanks."

Once in the bathroom, I stripped off my clothes and threw them in my hamper. I loved my job as a welder, but it would be nice to come home sometimes and drop onto my couch without a shower, but it was necessary to get the dirt and stink off of me.

I was done in five minutes, and I quickly dressed before heading back to the kitchen. "What are you hungry for?"

I wasn't the best cook, but I probably beat whatever our mom was heating up on a spoon in the living room of her trailer.

"Pizza."

I looked over from the open fridge to see my brother grinning at me. He knew I didn't care for cooking either, and pizza was cheap and easy, so I almost always said yes to it.

"Fine. You win."

"It's not like I had to twist your arm."

"You're right." I pulled my phone from my back pocket and pulled up Spencer's favorite pizza place app to put in our usual order. While I waited, I peeked over at my brother to see he had returned to his book.

My brother was almost seventeen—sixteen years younger than me. He was a smart kid—smarter than me—and I hated that he had to put up with the home life that he had. Our mother was worthless, but she hadn't always been that way.

When I had been born, my parents hadn't had much to call their own, but we were happy. When I was nine, my parents were in a car accident. My father was killed, and my mother was permanently injured, so she couldn't work and went on disability. But she wasn't incapacitated enough for her to forget she'd previously been a loving mother, and she turned into someone who spent all her time with men and doing drugs.

When she got pregnant with Spencer, I actually thought she would turn her life around, but when

Spencer's dad left after he was three months old, she went back to her old ways. I had practically raised my brother until I graduated high school.

We ate pizza, and I helped Spencer with his homework, although *help* is a generous word. He had better grades than I had when I was his age.

We were just discussing watching a movie when the word *Mom* popped up on my brother's phone screen. We both groaned. If our mom was calling, it meant that she wanted something from Spence, and he had learned long ago not to ignore her phone calls.

"Shit. Marjorie's calling." I hadn't called that woman Mom in years.

His face was filled with disappointment as he picked up his cell. "Hey," he answered reluctantly.

"Where are you?" she bellowed loud enough that I could hear it from the other side of the table.

Spence sighed. "At Dom's."

"Get your ass home."

His shoulders slumped. "Okay."

"And grab me a case and a carton on your way."

I scoffed. Our mother had several places that allowed her minor son to pick up her alcohol and cigarettes. I wanted to call CPS and turn our mother in, but Spencer wouldn't let me. He didn't want any of the owners or employees of the stores he bought from to get in trouble.

"Okay," Spencer said again and hung up.

I gritted my teeth as I watched him pick up his books and stuff them in his backpack.

Once upon a time, I had tried to get custody of Spencer, but my mother wasn't having it. Even after I told her that she could keep the government checks and he would only sleep at my house, she wouldn't give in. Partly because she'd had one too many DUIs and she needed an errand boy and also because she was weirdly possessive of my brother.

I even went to a couple of lawyers, but most of them said my case was hopeless due to my criminal record. Unlike my brother, I hadn't had a safe haven to go to when I needed to get away from my house, so I'd hung out with my friends who weren't what you would call good role models.

So, even though my mother had been busted for drinking and driving, I had disorderly conduct, vandalism, and a misdemeanor assault on my record. And even though it had all happened over a decade ago, I had known it would hurt me if we went in front of a judge. Plus, the state seemed to favor the mother, especially over someone who wasn't a parent.

"Sorry, I have to go."

I shook my head. "This isn't your fault. Don't ever apologize for her. You just get home safely. Don't get pulled over by the cops."

"I always put Mom's stuff in the trunk."

I snorted. "Yeah, but they could still bust you."

"I'll be careful."

I walked Spencer to the door and ruffled his hair. "See you later, kid."

"See ya later, old man," he yelled as he ran out the door to his POS car.

Grinning, I stood and watched as my brother pulled out of the driveway and onto the road before shutting the door.

Once it was closed, I leaned back against it and sighed. I hated sending him back there.

My phone pinged in my pocket, and I pulled it out, ready to call Spencer and tell him not to text and drive but it wasn't him.

Gina: Thank you for the favor last night.

I snorted.

Me: Shouldn't I be thanking you?

Gina: I don't know. Was she even good, or did she lie there like a cold fish?

A cold fish Vivian was not. She'd needed help opening up, but I could still almost feel the way her hot pussy had felt, clamped on my dick. And don't even get me started on her taste. I could eat her every day.

Me: I don't kiss and tell.

Gina: Since when? I call bullshit. But either way, Suzie Stern actually had a smile on her face this morning. A smile.

Me: Suzie Stern?

Gina: Vivian's last name is Stern, so some coworkers and I gave her the nickname Suzie Stern. It's kind of like Negative Nancy. Not only is it her last name, but she's also always so serious. Except for today.

A slow smile spread across my face. It felt good to know I'd fucked a smile onto Vivian's face.

Me: Glad I could help. Just let me know when you need me again.

Gina: For real?

Me: Sure. Why not?

Gina: Because repeat hookups are not your thing. I figured if she asked me again, I'd find someone else.

Like hell.

Me: I'm not playing. If Vivian needs help again, you ask me first.

NINE

VIVIAN

WHEN I GOT BACK TO WORK ON MONDAY MORNING, I took the long way to my office, and before I went around every corner, I paused to make sure Mr. St. James wasn't there.

When his ex-wife had walked into the mayor's conference room, I'd thought for sure he had sent me there to get information on her. I half-expected him to be waiting for me in my office when I got back to the firm.

He hadn't been, and I hadn't seen him the rest of the day.

I was beginning to suspect Mr. St. James was playing the long game, so he wouldn't look suspicious to me. But it didn't matter if he was playing any game; I did not want to be a spy for him even if he was a name partner and had a lot of control over my future in the firm.

Not only had it been obvious that Delaney St. James and the mayor were friends, but she'd also seemed like a nice person. She was a family court judge, so I hadn't worked with her in a professional sense, but she treated Rayne and me like we were her equals. I'd had many judges talk down to me like I wasn't intelligent or as if they were better than me, so it was a nice change.

Once the initial meeting was over, I felt uncomfortable that I hadn't told her who I worked for when the mayor asked us to introduce ourselves. But I hadn't wanted her to think I was there to spy on her either. While working together on a project wasn't the same as lawyer-client confidentiality, which was sacred, I didn't want anyone to question my ethics by thinking I was a snitch.

The door to my office loomed close. I hastened my last few steps, and I sighed with relief once I passed the threshold. I had made it without seeing Mr. St. James, but it was going to get old real fast if I didn't come up with some kind of plan other than avoiding him.

"How did it go on Friday?" a voice said behind me, and I jumped.

With my hand on my chest, I swung around to see the very person I had been trying to dodge.

I supposed I could have tried to avoid him all I wanted, but he knew where my office was, and I couldn't change that.

I swallowed hard. "It was fine. Good. It was good," I practically stammered.

He took a sip of his coffee. "Good," he said with a nod.

I frowned in confusion. *That's it? He's not going to ask about his ex?*

"How was meeting the mayor?" he asked with a smile.

Uh...

I twisted my hands, waiting for the big question, figuring he was warming me up before he asked what he really wanted to know. "Good. A little bit surreal. She is the mayor after all."

"She's a good woman. I wouldn't be worried about working with her." Mr. St. James took another drink of his coffee. "And how were the other women you are working with?"

Here it was. The reason he had shown up.

"They were both lovely. I think we'll get along for the duration of the project."

If he was going to be vague with questions, I was going to be vague with my answers. Even though I'd planned to tell him nothing about his ex, I was going to make him come right out and ask before I told him I wasn't giving him any information on Delaney.

He smiled. "Glad to hear it. I admit, I felt a little guilty about sending you over there at the last minute. I know it's not something you were looking forward to, so I appreciate it. And whenever you need time off for this project, you can have it. If you need help with cases, let me know."

I lifted my chin. "That's good because I'm meeting them for lunch today."

Why I'd told him that, I didn't know. Because now, he knew I was going to see his ex-wife again.

"All right. Do you need anyone to help you with anything while you're gone?"

"No."

"Great." He lifted his mug. "Why don't you get some coffee? You deserve it."

And with that, he walked away.

I sprinted to the door to see if he was going to turn around and come back, but by this time, he was halfway down the hall. It was then that I realized he must not know I was working with his wife. And I didn't know what he would do if he found out.

Which only meant one thing.

I now had to keep it a secret from both of them that I was working with the other.

As if I didn't have enough things to worry about.

Around noon, I walked into the restaurant where I was meeting Delaney and Rayne with a cloud of unease hanging over my head.

I needed this project to go smoothly, and while I didn't want to do it, I realized Mr. St. James was right. It would look good to the partners, and if they didn't want me as a partner when the time came to decide, it would look good on my résumé when I sought out a new firm. And if it was going to go well, I didn't need any drama.

I decided that I wasn't going to tell either one of them I was working with their ex. If they asked, I wouldn't lie, but if they didn't ask, they would never have to know. It was best for everyone involved.

"Good afternoon. May I help you?" asked the woman at the hostess stand.

"I'm meeting a couple people. The table is under St. James," I told her.

"I'm here too," a breathless voice said behind me, and I turned to see Rayne hurrying toward me.

"This way, please. Ms. St. James is here."

Rayne and I followed the hostess to our table. When Delaney saw us, she smiled and stood.

"Hello, ladies," she said.

"Hello," both of us responded at the same time. Rayne laughed at our double greeting.

"Have either of you been here before?" Delaney asked after we both were seated and our menus were handed to us.

"No," I said, and Rayne shook her head.

Delaney rolled her eyes in pleasure. "Mmm. Pretty much every pasta dish on this menu is good. You can't go wrong."

Rayne bit her lip. "I love pasta, but I'm trying to lower my carb intake."

I wrinkled my nose. "Whatever for?"

Rayne's eyes shot to mine.

"I apologize," I said and rolled my eyes. "My sister says that I sometimes need to be more tactful."

Rayne sighed. "Are we all friends now?" She looked at Delaney and me. "It feels like if we're going to be spending a lot of time together, we're going to be friends."

I shrugged, but Delaney said, "Sure." She smiled. "It's the start of a beautiful friendship."

Rayne grinned back. "I'm eating fewer carbs. If it were up to me, that's all I would eat, but I am trying to have a more balanced diet. My father was diagnosed with type 2 diabetes, and I don't want to wait until it happens to me."

Delaney leaned forward. "And..."

I looked back and forth. How had Delaney known there was an *and* to this?

Rayne blushed. "Oh, I don't know if I should say anything else. It's kind of personal."

"Now, you have to tell us," Delaney said.

I admit, my curiosity was very piqued. "What happens with Women in Law stays at Women in Law," I said, borrowing the old Vegas slogan.

Delaney snapped her fingers and pointed at me. "What Vivian said."

Rayne rolled her eyes. "Okay, but know that I am super embarrassed, so I'm trusting both of you not to make fun of me."

Delaney held out her little finger. "Pinkie promise."

Rayne held up her pinkie, too, but stopped and looked at me.

"Oh." I mimicked them, and we all clasped our fingers together in a promise.

"I've put on a few pounds—a few pounds I didn't need in the first place—and since then, my boyfriend doesn't seem to be as interested in sex anymore."

Rayne was what society considered plus-size, but

society sucked. She was beautiful, and her boyfriend probably didn't deserve her.

"If he doesn't like you when you've gained weight, he's not worth keeping," I blurted out.

"Uh...thanks for the advice," she said in a tone that said she was not thankful. "But he has never commented on my weight. It's just the only thing that's changed, and it sucks."

"Have you tried talking to him?" Delaney asked.

That was probably a much better response than mine.

"Yes, and no. I've brought up the sex thing, but not my weight. He told me he's been busy with work and he's been tired lately."

Delaney curled her lips. "This is why I'm so glad I'm divorced." But a slow smile spread across her face in a way that I wasn't sure if she was even aware it was happening. "Although our problem was never bedroom stuff." She closed her eyes, and a small shiver went through her.

When she looked at Rayne and me again, she caught us both staring at her. I was sure Rayne was curious, but not as much as me. I shouldn't want to know what Preston St. James was like in bed, but I did. Not because I wanted to be with him. No, it was simply because I was intrigued.

Delaney cleared her throat. "Sorry. Anyway, maybe you should try talking to your boyfriend again."

Rayne shrugged. "Maybe." She turned toward me. "What's your story? Delaney's divorced, I'm in a relationship, but what about you?"

"Oh, I'm single. I had a serious boyfriend for quite a

few years, but we recently broke up when we decided our lives were headed in different directions."

"I'm sorry," Rayne said.

"I'm not. It was for the best."

"So, I'm getting advice from two women who aren't sleeping with anyone."

An image of a naked Dominick sprang to mind, and this time, I was the one who shivered.

TEN

VIVIAN

SINCE MY LUNCH MEETING WITH DELANEY AND Rayne at the beginning of the week, I hadn't been able to think about much of anything other than sex with Dominick.

It was just that...it had been *so* good.

Even though the guy wasn't my type and I would never date someone like him, I couldn't stop thinking about his dick.

It was Friday, meaning that it had only been a week since we'd slept together, and I already wanted to do it again. Last time I'd felt like this, the restless feeling had taken three months to build. It was quite a jump from that to one week.

It was a good thing I had a meeting in ten minutes. Being face-to-face with a client would help me focus on work.

Just then, my phone rang, the caller ID telling me it was the front desk.

"This is Vivian," I answered.

"Hi, Vivian. It's Mara. Your one thirty called to cancel."

"Now?" I said out of frustration. "It's a little late. I could have been doing other things besides waiting for them to show up."

"I'm sorry," Mara said.

I sighed. "It's not your fault. Thanks for letting me know." I hung up the phone and pushed myself up off my chair.

I needed a file from another associate, and since my meeting had been canceled, I might as well work on that instead.

As I made my way down the hall, I was almost to the receptionist's desk, and for a second, I thought I saw Dominick in my peripheral vision. I did a double take, but the man had passed. I rushed to turn the corner, but all I saw were the elevator doors closing.

As I stood there, staring at nothing, I realized there was no way that he would be at my job. What would he be doing in a law firm?

Fuck. I had it bad.

I swung around and marched to Kirk Bauman's office.

"Kirk."

He looked up. "Oh, hey, Vivian."

"I need the Weber file."

Kirk smiled politely. "Oh, I took it back to Records."

My jaw clenched, and I took a deep breath. "I told you I needed it after you."

He frowned in fake sympathy. "Sorry. I forgot."

"Yeah, whatever," I muttered under my breath before turning and heading for Records.

If I were a man, I'd bet he wouldn't have "forgotten" that I needed it.

When I reached Gina's desk, I didn't offer a greeting. "I need the Weber file."

She looked at me like she couldn't believe I was asking for that. "I *just* put it away."

I held my hands up. "Don't blame me. Kirk forgot I needed it. Allegedly."

She sighed and headed into the room where everything was kept. Meanwhile, I tapped my toes as I tried to patiently wait. But it was hard when I was irritated and sexually frustrated. At that point, I wanted the day to be over, so I could leave work.

Maybe I'd get a massage or something.

I closed my eyes and imagined hands kneading the knots out of my neck. The hands would work out all the kinks before massaging my back. Then, maybe I would flip over, and the handsome man who was working on my body would accidentally pull off my towel and run his hands down—

"*Grr.*" I opened my eyes and stomped my feet. *Why was I turning my nice massage into something sexual?*

"Are you okay?" Gina asked, eyes wide.

And wasn't that just great? I hadn't realized she'd come back up to her desk and caught me mid-tantrum.

Stepping forward, I held out my hand. "I'm fine. Can I have that?" I asked, referring to the manila file folder in her hand.

She tilted her head and looked me up and down. "You don't seem fine."

"Just give me the file."

Gina gasped and grinned. "Do you need another dick appointment?" She nodded, as if she was answering her own question. "Yep, I bet that's exactly what you need."

I ground my teeth. "No, I do not."

"Come on. You can be real with me, Vivian."

With an impatient snort, I launched the upper half of my body over her desk and snatched the file from her hand. I spun on my heel and stormed away.

"Mara was right. You do need to get laid again."

At least, that was what I thought she'd said.

Abruptly, I stopped and scowled over my shoulder. "What did you say?"

"I was wondering if you have plans tonight."

"That's not what you said."

She rolled her eyes. "Just answer the question."

"Are you asking me to hang out?"

She scoffed. "God, no."

The feeling was mutual.

"Then, I'm doing nothing. Just the way I want it." I would probably do some work from home, but I doubted Gina considered that having plans.

"Good," she said, picking up her phone.

I sighed and rushed back to my office.

DOMINICK

I approached the man sitting at the table of the fancy restaurant I had just entered. He laughed at some sexist joke his friends had made, and I felt no guilt about what I was about to do.

But even though his assistant had given me the information of where he'd be at this time and he looked exactly like the profile picture I'd found on the internet, I still approached him and asked, "Ron Stewart?"

He turned toward me and eyed my too-casual clothes, my tattoos, and my nose ring. He chuckled to his friends like he couldn't believe someone like me had had the audacity to approach someone like him.

But I simply waited for him to answer me. I wasn't in a rush, and guys like him didn't intimidate me.

When he realized I wasn't going to leave, he sat up straighter in his chair and threw the napkin from his lap onto his empty plate. "Yeah, I'm Ron Stewart. What's it to ya?" He deliberately scanned me up and down. "I doubt you're here about hiring my company. You could never afford me."

He and his buddies all laughed.

"That's okay. I don't need to hire you."

"Oh, you don't, huh?" His voice was filled with arrogance. "Then, what are you here for?"

I pulled the envelope out of my jacket and dropped it in his lap. "I'm here to serve you." I smiled. "Have a good day."

As I strolled away, I heard Ron Stewart cussing at me, but I was used to the hate. No one liked a process server.

While I worked as a welder for ten hours a day, four days of the week, I did process serving on my other days. It helped me save up to take in my brother after he turned eighteen, and it gave me the flexibility many part-time jobs didn't.

When I got outside, my phone vibrated in my pocket, so I pulled it out to see who had texted me.

> Gina: Were you serious about helping out Vivian again?

The smile on my face morphed into a grin. What a coincidence. This side gig of mine was how I had met Gina.

> Me: Fuck yeah.

> Gina: Good. But you're going to have to go to her.

> Me: Whatever. I'm done for the day, so I can do that.

> Gina: Here's her address.

Gina sent a link to Google Maps.

Gina: But I have to warn you: she was in a bad mood at work today.

I laughed.

Me: Thanks for the heads-up.

If I was lucky, I would be able to fuck the bad mood right out of her.

ELEVEN
VIVIAN

When I got home that night, I put on a pair of leggings and a comfortable T-shirt, and I poured a glass of wine while I waited for my dinner to be delivered.

Even though I was away from the office, I got on my laptop. I couldn't bring files home from work, but I could do a few things away from the firm, like look over my schedule and organize in my mind what I had to do on Monday.

I was deep into my to-do list when there was a knock at my door. I looked at the time and saw that a half hour had passed. I wasn't even hungry, but I guessed my food had arrived.

I had paid with my credit card, but I liked to give my tips in cash because I didn't always trust companies to give it all to their drivers. I scooped up the money from my kitchen counter and opened the door.

The deliveryman was holding the food up in front of

his face, so I couldn't see what he looked like, but there was something familiar about him.

He rattled off my building number and street. "Apartment 216?" His voice was low, and it also seemed familiar, but I couldn't honestly tell, as my neighbors were opening their front door and stepping out into the hall.

"That's me."

I thought maybe he had been reading the receipt taped to the bag, but he didn't lower it after I confirmed he had the right place.

And since it had been established that I had a short fuse, it didn't take me long to get impatient.

"Look, if you don't hand over my food in the next few seconds, I'm keeping your damn tip."

My neighbors, a couple in their fifties, gasped at my rudeness.

The bag lowered to show a laughing Dominick. "Shit, Viv, I heard you were in a mood, but I didn't expect this. And you can keep your money. You can pay me in orgasms instead."

"Oh my God," one of the neighbors said, and I realized I needed to get Dom out of the hallway.

I fisted his shirt in my hand and pulled him inside my apartment and slammed the door.

"What are you doing here?"

He raised his eyebrows. "Isn't it obvious? I'm bringing you your food." He looked behind me and headed for the kitchen once he spotted it.

"I've never seen you here before," I said suspiciously.

"That's because I don't actually deliver food."

"Then, what do you do?" I challenged.

"I'm a welder. I just happened to see your delivery guy in the hallway and took it from him."

"Please tell me you tipped him," I said as Dom started unpacking my order.

"Of course I paid him."

I let out a breath of relief. Knowing how little those employees made, I always tried to give them an extra-good tip.

"Here's the money to pay you back," I said, sliding the money on the counter over to him.

He stared down at the money and then up at me. "I told you, you can pay me in orgasms. Besides, I gave him more than that."

I crossed my arms over my chest. "What makes you think I'm going to have sex with you again in order for you to get those orgasms?" I knew I was being difficult. The idea of getting naked again with Dominick didn't sound half-bad, but I stubbornly wanted to hang on to my bad mood. "What are you even doing here anyway? I didn't invite you."

"Oof." He put his hand to his chest, like he was in pain. "That one hurt."

"You know what I mean. How do you know where I live?" I narrowed my eyes. "How do I know I can trust you?"

He tilted his head. "How hungry are you?"

Huh? What does that have to do with anything?

"Only a little." I dropped a hand on the counter and leaned forward. *"Why are you here?"* I said, making sure to enunciate each word clearly.

He came around to my side of the counter, and I dropped my hand and straightened my spine. He moved in close but didn't touch me.

"A little bird told me that you needed me. She's also the one who gave me your address."

I frowned. He had to be referring to Gina. She'd asked me if I needed another dick appointment, but I'd told her no, and she also had access to my address from work. And, now, here was Dominick, standing in my kitchen.

"So, Gina sent you. I don't understand what she gets out of helping me."

Dom licked his lips and grinned.

"I mean, what she gets out of doing something that *she thinks* is helpful," I quickly added.

He shrugged. "Because you're friends."

"No. Gina and I are not friends."

"Maybe she wants to be."

"Why?"

He laughed. "Man, you are hard on yourself."

"Whatever." I wasn't going to argue with him about this. I would figure it out on my own. "It doesn't matter anyway because you need to leave."

"I will on one condition."

I crossed my arms again. "What's that?"

He looked around until his eyes settled on my food,

and he put a finger on one of the square takeout boxes. "What's in here?"

"A calzone."

He gently tugged my arms down. "The condition is, you let me kiss you, and if you want me to stop, you say *calzone*."

"Why wouldn't I just say no?"

"Because sometimes, we say no when we mean yes, and I don't want to stop unless you really want me to." He smiled. "Besides, this way is more fun."

I rolled my eyes. "Fine. Calzone."

He tsked. "You can't say it until after I start kissing you."

"All right. Kiss me then."

Putting his hands on my hips, he yanked me to him. "What's the safe word again?" he whispered.

I opened my mouth, but I couldn't remember. His hard length was pushing against the seam of my pants. I could barely recall a single word with him so close.

"That's what I thought," he said in a deep voice as his mouth lowered to mine.

TWELVE
DOMINICK

My plan was to take it slow. A gentle kiss to give Vivian a chance to see how she really felt. But two seconds after my lips brushed against hers, she launched herself into my arms and attacked me. In a good way.

Make that a *great* way.

I knew she had been horny the last time because it had been a while since she'd had sex. This time was different. She knew I could get her where she wanted to go, so she specifically wanted me to get her there rather than some random dude.

Her eyes were closed as she wrapped her arms around my neck and moaned. I'd enjoyed the woman who stood in my bedroom like she was afraid to get dirty, but I liked this version of her even more. All of this suddenly released passion had me ready to go.

Unexpectedly, she backed away, and I figured this was where she was going to pull herself together and tell me to get out. I had no intention of letting her stop unless she used that little safe word. I wanted this to happen, and I knew she wanted it too. But it turned out, no safe word came out of her mouth.

She shocked me by pushing me backward toward the living room. I took a moment to look around at her place. Her home was definitely classier than mine. Mine had more personality, yet her apartment suited her.

The hard shove pushing me down onto the couch brought the direction of my thoughts back to her and the look of pure lust on her face. Sliding down to the floor, she unzipped my fly and worked my shaft out of my boxers with her soft fist.

I hissed and then held my breath as I waited to see what she planned to do next. I knew what I wanted her to do, but waiting to see if she liked the same things I did was killing me.

She gripped the length of my cock with one hand and moved my foreskin back with the other until I was exposed to her gaze. Her lips slipped over my head, and I groaned.

I'd been hard since I had seen her, but watching her on her knees wasn't something I'd thought would happen, and while I had known I'd enjoy it, I hadn't realized I'd like it this much. She worked the head of my cock with her mouth, which was driving me out of my fucking mind.

Both of her hands stroked me, and I watched her take as much of my length as she could into her mouth. As fiercely as she'd attacked my mouth in the kitchen, she was just as hungry when it came to my cock. I put my hands on her head and rocked my hips just a little to see if she'd like that. The moan that filled the room flipped my switch hard, and the vibration it made on my dick drew my balls up tight.

I knew I was getting close, and if I wanted to make sure Vivian came before me, I needed to end this before I made a mess in her mouth.

I groaned at the thought of doing just that, then pulled her mouth off me anyway.

She released my cock with a soft pop of suction and frowned in confusion as she stood.

"Take your clothes off," I demanded with a lift of my chin.

"You're bossy. You'd better be careful, or I'll use the safe word."

I snagged her around the waist and pushed my hand between her legs. Even through her leggings, I could feel she was hot and wet. "You could use it," I said with a smirk, "but then you won't get to come either."

"Fine. Take off your clothes," she said, throwing my words back at me as her T-shirt was yanked off and tossed to the side.

I grinned. "Now, who's bossy?"

She flashed me a cocky smile. "My house, my rules."

I made quick work of my clothes and rolled a condom on my aching dick in record time. The way this was going, we were going to be fucking before either of us thought of this step. The woman was on fire, and I was barely finished before she hopped on me.

"Whoa," I said as I caught her as she straddled me.

This behavior she was displaying was aggressive and uncontrolled. The first one, I had no doubts she had that in excess, but the second one, I didn't think she showed it too often. It was hot as hell.

The sexy smile had an added challenge as she grabbed my cock and rubbed it between her folds. I could feel the grip of her pussy as she welcomed me into her heat. Her hands grabbed my shoulders as she sank down like she was savoring each and every inch.

It was the sweetest torture to watch her sexy body as she drew me inside, and I had to do everything in my power not to blow my load. When I was so far inside her that her ass touched my balls, she made one small rotation with her hips.

"Fuck." I grabbed her hips and lifted her, so her tight nipples were close enough for me to draw one between my lips.

The bud seemed to grow more rigid as I pulled it between my teeth. She fisted my hair and pulled me closer as she rocked herself on my length.

Moving to the other side, I gave the other nipple the same treatment.

"Yes. Yes, please." She panted her words, and I worked her nipple with my tongue before nipping it between my teeth and licking the sting away.

The last time we had been together, I hadn't gotten to see the expression that crossed her face when she reached her climax, and part of me had regretted it.

This time, I wanted to watch her come on my cock. The moment of no return. When the grinding lost the rhythm and nothing mattered more than her attaining her satisfaction.

That was what I wanted to witness.

As she grew closer, I helped her ride me, loving her responsiveness as she moved. Her back arched, and the moment I'd been waiting for arrived. Her eyes closed, her lips parted, and I couldn't stop watching her, anticipating her climactic finish.

Her nails sank into my back as she drew close. That move, coupled with the way her pussy gripped my cock like the best hand job, was almost enough to bring me to an end, too, but I wasn't going to let that happen.

I was torn between grabbing her hips and rocking her clit against me or using my thumb to rub against her. I chose the latter because I wanted to make sure I could watch her come apart. Her breaths hitched a few times before she froze for a second. I held my breath and waited for the tsunami of pleasure to start.

The woman didn't disappoint as the waves of her release caused her to squeeze my cock even harder as she reached her peak. Her flushed face went from scrunched in concentration of reaching completion to her teeth biting her bottom lip.

Making sure my partner had an orgasm hadn't ever been my issue, but holding back this time was one of the harder things I'd ever done in my life, and then a whimper from her did me in. I would rather have had her scream my name, but for now, I'd take anything but silence. And the little noise she made as she finished ricocheted me through the roof. I gripped her hips and fucked myself into her until I roared through my climax.

I wasn't sure which way was up when I was done, but in the end, I laid my head back against the couch as she collapsed against my chest.

Our breathing grew regular, and my chest cooled when she removed her body heat. I opened my eyes and found her staring at me with a strange expression on her face. She was studying my tattoos, but the real surprise was that she looked kind of happy.

Her eyes lifted to mine, but she didn't say a word.

"Is this the part where you kick me out?" I asked.

The corner of her mouth tilted up. "Tempting, but no."

"Then, what are you thinking?"

She squeezed her pussy around my shaft and smiled. "Wanna go again?"

My dick jumped at the thought as I groaned, but I needed another minute.

I kissed her and whispered, "Calzone."

THIRTEEN
DOMINICK

The next morning, I went to the park to meet Spencer with a smile on my face as memories of last night still ran through my head.

My brother and I met up to play basketball a few times a month as long as the weather was above fifty degrees. And since summer was right around the corner, Spencer and I were trying to start up our old routine.

I arrived before my brother, and since I was the one who brought the basketball, I shot some hoops while I was waiting for him to get there. But it wasn't long before I realized he was running really late. He was a teenager, so I didn't expect him to show up on time, but fifteen minutes had passed.

I checked my phone. He hadn't called or texted, so I rang him, a little annoyed that he'd forgotten about me or that he was too careless to let me know he wasn't coming. But his cell went straight to voice mail, which didn't sit well with me. Spencer was sixteen years old. He *always* had his phone on.

I called him again, just to make sure that it wasn't a glitch, and headed for my car. I could go home and wait for him to get ahold of me, or I could keep trying to call him. But my gut told me something might be seriously wrong, so I did the one thing I absolutely hated to do.

I pulled out of the parking lot and headed for my mom's place.

I pounded on the front door of my mother's trailer home. Even though it was late morning, there was a strong chance she wouldn't be awake. It all depended on how much she'd drunk last night and how late she'd stayed up.

Just as I was raising my fist again, the door swung open, and the woman who'd birthed me stood on the other side. She was only fifty-five years old, but she looked like she was eighty.

She had to squint in the bright sunlight, but once she realized it was me, she scowled. "What d'ya want?" she croaked, her voice harsh from her smoking at least a pack of cigarettes a day since she had been a teenager.

"Where's Spencer?"

"How the fuck would I know?"

"Because he's your son."

"He's sixteen."

I wasn't in the mood to argue with her.

"Listen, he's not answering his phone, and since this is his *home* and you are his *mother*, he should either be here or you should know where he is."

It was taking everything in me not to reach out and shake her. She wouldn't let Spencer live with me, but she sure as shit didn't care if he was okay or not.

"Let the kid in, Marjorie," a masculine voice said from inside the trailer.

She scoffed but opened the door farther to let me in. "He hasn't been a kid in a long time."

I pushed past her and her latest boyfriend to the back, where my brother's room was. Knocking, I said, "Spence, it's me," as I turned the knob and slipped inside.

The room was dark, but there was enough light for me to see my brother in his bed.

"Dammit, Spencer, you had me worried when you didn't show up this morning."

He didn't move, so I went to the bedside and shook him awake.

Spencer immediately winced and hissed before rolling onto his back.

"What's wrong?" I asked.

He blinked up at me. "Dom?"

"Yeah, it's me."

"What are you doing here?"

"We were supposed to play basketball this morning, but you didn't show. And your phone's dead or turned off."

"Sorry. I'll call you later."

I frowned. Spencer was acting odd.

"I'm here, so why don't I take you to breakfast? I'm sure Marjorie has nothing good out there, waiting for you."

"I'm not hungry."

"What is up with you?" I went over to the window and yanked the string on the blinds down, and then I marched back over to my brother. "Look at me."

He slowly met my eyes, and once he did, I noticed his pupils were still dilated despite the brightness.

I'd always dreaded this day, but I'd had high hopes it wouldn't come. "What the fuck did you take?"

"Nothing."

"Don't fucking lie to me. *What are you on?*"

He looked away. "Oxy."

I ran my hands through my hair in frustration. "Spence. What were you thinking?" Slicing my hand through the air, I said, "Never mind." I knew what he had probably been thinking. He'd probably been thinking that if his mom was doing drugs, he might as well be too.

Been there, done that.

I threw back the covers. "Get up." I grabbed on to his arm to help him up.

"*Ow,*" he yelled.

I dropped his hand like it was on fire and studied my brother. He rolled away from me as he cried in pain.

Suddenly, I had a whole new take on the situation.

"Spencer, I'm going to ask you one question, and I want an honest answer."

"Okay," he muttered.

"Did you take the oxy because you're in pain?"

"Yes."

"Do you need to go to the hospital?"

"I—I think so."

"Fuck," I cursed under my breath, low enough that I hoped he couldn't hear. "Did Mom do this to you?"

"You said one question."

He didn't have to respond. I already knew the answer.

"Yeah...yeah, I guess I did." I took a calming breath. "Can you look at me?"

Spencer slowly turned back to face me.

"I'm going to help you out of here, and I'm not going to let anyone hurt you." I raised my eyebrows. "Okay?"

He nodded. "Okay."

FOURTEEN
DOMINICK

THE DOCTOR STEPPED INTO THE ER ROOM MY brother and I had been waiting in for the last half hour.

"Mr. Reyes, it looks like your arm is broken," she told Spencer.

It was hard, but I maintained my cool, for my brother's sake and for the doctor's. I had lied and told them Spencer was my son. Since he was under eighteen, I didn't want to risk them calling Marjorie. I was worried they wouldn't give him the care he needed if she didn't come to the hospital, so I had lied and was ready to sign any forms I had to in order to get a cast on his arm.

I also didn't want to overreact in case she thought I might have been the one to break Spencer's arm.

"Will I have to have surgery?" Spencer asked.

Panic rushed through me. "Surgery?" It was one thing to hide the truth to get a cast. It was another thing to lie in order to get an operation.

"Yeah. A kid at school broke his arm and had to have surgery."

I whipped my head in the doctor's direction, pleading with my eyes for her to tell us no.

"No surgery."

"Thank fuck." I cleared my throat. "I mean, thank God."

The doctor smiled for a second at my swearing, but her face went back to serious. "You're lucky. But you need to be careful. And you shouldn't have waited to come in. If your...*dad* hadn't forced you to come now, I would have probably had a different answer by the time you did come in."

"Yes, ma'am."

"I'm going to have the nurse bring in the supplies to cast your arm, and then we might have to do another X-ray to confirm that everything is where it should be."

Spencer nodded.

"Thank you, Doctor," I said.

She closed the door behind her, and I stared at my brother.

"You promised to tell me what happened if it was broken," I said in a firm voice.

Spence had been avoiding telling me what had happened last night, saying it wasn't a big deal. But I'd told him a fracture was a huge deal, so he'd agreed to give me all the details if I was right about the status of his arm.

He looked away and sighed. "Mom and I got into a fight."

"Okay. About what?"

"Does it matter?"

I scoffed. "Considering what the outcome was, yes."

"She's late in paying the electricity...again."

My mouth tightened into a thin line. "How often does this happen?"

Spencer shrugged. "I don't know. Every few months."

Now, my jaw clenched. "Has it ever been shut off?"

"A couple of times."

"Why don't you tell me these things? I can help."

He scowled at me. "Because you shouldn't have to. It's not your home or your responsibility. It's hers."

"I know," I said in a gentle voice. "But not holding our mother accountable for her actions means you suffer."

"Like I said, it doesn't happen all the time."

I didn't say anything more about Marjorie not paying the bills because I didn't want to upset Spencer further. He already had too much to deal with as a sixteen-year-old.

"I'm letting it go." *For now.* "Can you tell me what else happened?"

"Mom gave Mitch a load of cash to go to the liquor store."

"Is Mitch the loser who was sitting in the living room this morning?"

Spencer smiled at my insult. "Yeah."

"Got it."

"Anyway, I reminded her she hadn't paid the bill yet and that it was overdue. She ignored me, so I tried to take the money from Mitch."

My spine straightened. "He didn't do this to you, did he?"

Spencer snorted. "Mitch? No. He's a piece of shit, but he pretty much lets Mom run the show."

I relaxed a little. Because if Mitch had touched my brother, I wasn't sure I would be able to not touch him back. And I would give him more than a broken arm.

"So, Mom didn't like that. She needs her drinks, you know. And she got mad and pushed me as I was mid-step. I lost my balance and fell against the counter. I heard a snap, and I'm pretty sure Mom and Mitch heard it, too, because she started to cry and begged me not to call the police."

And knowing my kindhearted brother, I knew *he'd* felt bad for her.

"She shoved some pills in my hand and told me to go sleep it off. And I was in so much pain that I just wanted it to go away."

I wanted to yell and shake my mother. No amount of sleep was going to fix a broken arm.

I put my hand on Spencer's good arm. "It's okay. I don't blame you. But please, if something like this ever happens again, call me."

"I didn't want to bother you."

"I don't care." Okay, I kind of did. Having to suddenly leave Vivian when I was deep inside her would have sucked, but my brother meant more to me than sex. "You are more important to me. You're my brother."

"What's going to happen now?"

"You mean, am I going to go and yell at our mother?" I asked.

"Yeah."

"I would if I thought it would do any good."

That bitch didn't care what I thought. I could only hope she felt guilty when I brought Spencer home with a cast on his arm.

"Are you going to call family services?"

The knob on the hospital room door twisted, and a voice said, "Knock, knock," before it was pushed open all the way.

Spencer's nurse pushed in a cart with medical supplies on it. And that was the end of the *family services* conversation.

"Looks like someone's getting a cast," the nurse said.

"Yeah," Spencer said, giving her a small smile.

The nurse looked around, and I realized she was assessing the lack of space in the room.

I stood. "I can get out of here if you need me to," I offered.

"I'm sure Spencer would appreciate his dad being in the room for this, but if you wouldn't mind stepping out while I move some things around, that would be great."

I nodded. "No problem." I turned to my brother. "I'll be right outside."

As I stepped out, the doctor approached me with steady eyes. I was sure she was taking in my appearance now that Spencer's bed wasn't blocking me and I wasn't sitting down.

"How did you say your son broke his arm again?" she asked.

"I didn't." If she was trying to get me to tell her I did it, she was wasting her time. But I didn't fault her for doing her job. In fact, I appreciated it. "I only found out after you left the room. He wouldn't tell me what happened until it was confirmed his arm was broken."

She narrowed her eyes and clutched both ends of her stethoscope in her hands. "And how did it happen?"

"I think you should ask him, but I'll give you a hint. It has something to do with ou—his mother."

"You know, I know you're not his father."

I raised my eyebrows. "Oh?"

"Yeah." She looked around. "But you don't have to worry. I won't tell."

"But that's the thing, Doctor. Once you talk to my brother"—since she had figured it out, I might as well admit it—"I hope you do tell."

She nodded in understanding.

Family services would be a lot more likely to look into my brother if an emergency room physician called.

At least, I was really hoping they would.

FIFTEEN
DOMINICK

WHEN I BROUGHT MY BROTHER HOME, THE TRAILER was empty.

"Go pack a bag. You're going to stay with me for a few days."

"What about Mom?" What Spencer meant was, *Mom isn't going to say yes to this.*

"I'll handle her when the time comes. You go pack." I was hoping we'd be gone by the time she came home, and then I would only have to deal with her over the phone.

Spencer headed to his room while I looked around. Everything was pretty much the same as when I had grown up there, except there were a few more holes in the furniture, more stains on the walls, and the TV was newer and flatter. It would be pretty hard to watch that television without any electricity.

There was a bunch of papers on the kitchen table, and

I rummaged through them, hoping to locate the electric bill. It took a little digging, but I managed to find it.

"How's it going back there?" I shouted down the hall.

"Fine. I'm not as fast with one arm."

I winced. "I'll be there in a minute." Quickly, I pulled out my phone and found the website for the electric company.

Just as I hit Send to pay the bill, my brother said, "No need. I'm finished." He looked at the paper in my hand and to my phone. "What are you doing?"

"Nothing." I threw the bill on the table and tucked my phone in my back pocket. "You have everything you need?"

"Yeah."

"What about your school stuff for Monday?"

His eyes widened. "I'm staying longer than the weekend?"

"If I have my way, yes."

"Okay." He let his duffel bag slide off his shoulder. "But you know it's probably not going to happen, right?" he said on his way back to his room.

I didn't answer because we both knew he was right.

Just as Spencer and I were putting his stuff in my car, my mom and her boyfriend pulled up.

She flung open the passenger door. "What are you doing?" she accused as she stormed over to us.

Spencer instinctively got behind me. Even though he was now taller and bigger, he was still scared of our mother, and it only made me more determined to get him out of there.

"I'm taking Spencer to stay with me for a few days."

"The hell you are. He's my son."

Her boyfriend slowly came around the front of his truck but stayed back and didn't seem to even want to intervene.

"Yeah, well, he's my brother, and I'm going to take him somewhere he will be safe."

Marjorie scoffed. "He's safe here."

I stepped to the side and picked up my brother's arm. "Oh, was he safe when you broke his arm? Or how about when you shoved a bunch of illegal prescription pills at him and told him to sleep it off?"

I took way too much satisfaction from seeing the guilt wash over her face, but I wanted her to feel bad. I wanted her to realize what a shitty parent she was.

She moved forward. "I'm sorry, baby. Mama didn't mean to."

"I know," Spencer mumbled.

"Why don't we go inside? Mama will make you some soup."

I put myself in front of Spencer again. "Soup isn't going to fix what you did. Also, you and I both know there's no soup in there," I said with a nod toward her home. "You're just going to drink your lunch and leave Spencer to fend for himself."

She swung fast, but I was faster, and I caught her hand before she slapped me.

"You don't want to do that," I said in a low voice. "I'm *so close* to calling the cops on you for what you did to Spence."

Panic flooded her face.

"Here's what you're going to do," I told her. "You're going to let Spencer stay with me for a few days, and you aren't going to call him or text him or contact him in any way. He's tired, and he needs rest. If you do that, maybe, just maybe, I will let him come back home."

"I'm still his mother," she spat out.

"Then, fucking act like it." I threw her arm at her and spun away. "Get in the car, Spencer," I said as I strode to the driver's side.

Marjorie's eyes darted between Spencer and me. I could sense she was freaking out that he was leaving.

Just as Spencer went to close his door, she yanked it back open. "If you go with Dominick, I'm going to sell your car."

Spencer's eyes flew to mine. He was the one in a panic now because he didn't want to leave his car behind for her to sell, and we both knew he couldn't drive right now. The ER doctor had given him pain meds—legitimate pain meds —and he wasn't supposed to be driving.

"Don't worry about her," I said in a steady voice.

Her threat was an empty one, but even if it wasn't, I would get a friend to help me get it later.

Spencer turned back to Marjorie and tugged the door from her grasp. "I gotta go, Mom. I'll see you in a few days."

It felt good to know that my brother trusted me as we drove off.

I closed the door to my brother's room. He had gone to bed an hour ago, but I'd wanted to make sure he was sleeping before I left to do a few things.

I snagged my keys from the table and headed for my car. I considered calling a friend to help me. Tony had even said he was around if I needed him. But the thing about Tony or most of my other friends was that none of them could help me with the thing I needed the most.

Tonight, there was only one person for that job.

SIXTEEN
VIVIAN

I PULLED THE WASHCLOTH AWAY FROM MY FACE AND perked up my ears.

Did I hear something, or was it one of my neighbors?

I waited, but when there was nothing, I finished washing my face, turned off the water, and hung up the cloth to dry.

Shutting the light off as I walked out, I heard a noise. It was my front door.

I glanced at the clock to see it was after ten as I hurried out of my bedroom. I suspected I had heard someone knocking the first time, and I didn't want whoever had shown up so late to leave, figuring it had to be something important.

Even with the urgency running through my veins, I used the peephole before I let in whoever was out there. I was surprised to see Dominick on the other side. After having sex on my couch last night, he'd gotten dressed, kissed me good-bye, and left despite it still being early in the evening. I hadn't expected him back here so soon.

However, the joking guy who I'd found standing outside my door yesterday was not the same man who was in my hallway tonight. He looked grim, seriousness written all over his face.

I swung open the door, and Dominick immediately pulled me into his arms and swept his tongue into my mouth. One of his strong hands was wrapped around my back as the other gripped my ass.

I didn't like sleeping in underwear, and I could feel how hard he was through the thin layer of my pajama pants.

I went from getting ready for bed to getting ready for sex in an embarrassingly short amount of time.

When Dominick set me back on my feet, I was breathless and unsure of what day it was.

"Damn, Viv, I got you moaning so loud that the neighbors are going to start coming out of their apartments," he said with the first hint of a smile. He grabbed both sides of the door trim and leaned forward, his white T-shirt stretching over his chest muscles. "If I didn't need your help right now, I would take you into your bedroom and fuck you until you screamed my name."

I sucked in a breath but managed to say, "I don't scream."

"Yet." He kissed me and backed up. "But in all seriousness, I need you to put on some shoes and come with me."

I looked down at myself. I was wearing a pair of PJs

that weren't revealing, but the pink and black pattern gave away that they were pajamas. Plus, there was a bigger problem. Two of them actually. "I'm not wearing a bra."

"Oh, believe me, I noticed." Dominick licked his bottom lip and glanced down at my chest before his eyes moved back up to mine. "But your sweet nipples are going to have to wait. And you'll be fine. We're not going anywhere in public."

I hesitated. "Promise?"

"Promise. If anything changes, I will buy you a bra myself."

For some reason, I chose to trust him. "Okay, but I still think I should change," I said as I went in search of some shoes.

"There's no point because you won't be wearing anything for very long," it sounded like he muttered.

I turned around. "What?"

"Nothing." He motioned with his hand. "Just put something on your feet, so we can go."

I slipped on my shoes and grabbed my purse as I pulled out my keys. "Where are we going?" I asked as I locked the dead bolt on my door.

"My mom's."

I had a silent mental freak-out when Dominick said I was going with him to his mother's house but only for a second.

The look on his face let me know this wasn't something he was looking forward to.

When we pulled up to a run-down trailer, I realized even more how different Dominick and I were.

"Is this where your mother lives?" I asked.

"Yeah. Home sweet home," he said, his voice full of disdain.

I'd spent most of my life in a nice two-story home in a middle-class neighborhood. And while I'd had a couple friends from school who lived in trailer homes, they had been well kept and clean.

The place Dominick had grown up had seen much better days a long time ago. The paint was peeling and caked in years' worth of dirt, screens were ripped off windows, and one window was covered with cardboard.

I was almost afraid to get out, and I was ashamed for thinking that about Dominick's childhood home.

Rubbing my hands over my thighs, I asked, "Okay, what do you need me to do?"

"Not much. I need you to drive before my mother wakes up and sees us."

I frowned. "That's it?" I put my hand on his arm, stopping him. "Wait. I'm not going to be some getaway driver, am I?"

He looked at me and laughed. "No," he said with a shake of his head. "I just need to get my brother's car."

I looked over the dash at the old car parked by the trailer home. "We're not stealing it, are we?"

Laughing again, he pushed open his car door. "Come

on, Bonnie. Let's get this over with before we get caught, breaking the law."

I scrambled out, rushed over to him, and put a hand on his chest. "Absolutely not. If I get caught, my career is over. Take me home. Right now."

Dominick threw his head back and laughed. Mystified by his reaction, I dropped my hand and stepped back, but he snaked his arm around my waist and kissed me. I was a sucker for his mouth because I melted into him, and I was so close to saying, *Fuck my career,* when he released me.

Putting his forehead to mine, he said, "We're not stealing anything. We're not doing anything illegal."

"Then, why do we need to do this before your mother sees us?"

"Because she's a fucking bitch, and the less I have to deal with her, the better." He stepped around me and slapped my ass, directing me to his vehicle. "You drive my car. I'll drive my brother's."

When we pulled up to his house, Dominick told me he needed to check on his brother and drop off his keys. He walked me inside, and I stood by the door to wait for him to take me back to my apartment.

He threw the keys on the small table by the front door and went down the hall. When he appeared again, in the same spot that I'd first seen him, memories flooded my mind of that night, and curiously, I found him even sexier tonight.

As he strode toward me, the look of determination on his face took my breath away. I knew it was in concern for his brother, but maybe that was what I found so attractive. He hadn't given me many details about why his brother was with him, except that he'd broken his arm, and it warmed my heart that Dominick was worried.

When he reached me, I held out his keys to him. "Are you ready?"

The corner of his mouth lifted into a half-smile. "I've been ready since I picked you up." He took his keys and tossed them next to his brother's.

"Wh—"

With one swift move, he put his shoulder in my belly and tossed me over it.

SEVENTEEN
VIVIAN

DOMINICK THREW ME ON HIS BED AND STARTED stripping out of his clothes.

One yank, and his shirt was gone.

I licked my lips, and my pussy clenched. "What are you doing?"

"Getting ready to fuck you." He grabbed one of my ankles and whipped my shoe into a corner. "I thought you understood how the night was going to end."

Thud.

There went my other shoe.

"What about your brother?"

"What about him?"

"You're being kind of loud. What if he hears us?" I asked as my pajama bottoms were stripped off me.

Dominick paused with the hem of my shirt in his hands. He tilted his head. "I thought you didn't make noise when you had sex, Vivian?"

"I don't, but you're throwing stuff around."

Yank.

My shirt was gone, and I was completely naked.

"My brother's on pain meds. He's not waking up for anything."

Dominick flicked his jeans open and pushed them off his hips. I couldn't help but stare at his dick as he kicked the denim off.

"I thought I was just doing you a favor tonight."

He lifted me up under my arms and tossed me toward the headboard. "You didn't think that was all I wanted from you, did you?"

"Well...yeah."

He smiled. "Vivian, we don't have that kind of relationship. You come to me for D appointments, remember?"

I leaned back on my elbows, stuck out my chest, and opened my legs. "You came to me last time...*remember?*" I said with a smirk.

"I'm a full-service kind of dude because that was still for you."

"But not tonight?"

He swiped his thumb over his bottom lip and used his other hand to grab his length. "Nope. Tonight, it's my V appointment."

"V appointment, huh?" I said almost more to myself than to him. "I would have thought you'd go with a P appointment."

He knelt on the bed and crawled toward me until he hovered over me, looking down on me. He trailed one hand from my collarbone to down my body. "Yeah, V appointment. *Vivian*...and *vagina*," he said, sinking two fingers inside me.

My inner muscles tightened around his digits, and I lifted my hips with a moan. "You almost—*almost*—made the V-word sound sexy." I grabbed on to my breasts and pinched my nipples while he worked me gently with his hand.

He leaned down to my ear. "How about *snatch*?"

I wrinkled my nose and shook my head.

"*Slit*?"

"I *hate* that word."

"Noted." He sucked in a breath. "How about...*pussy*? Is *pussy* better?"

"Much," I panted with a nod.

"Wait. I know." He chuckled. "*Cunt*. Viv, your fucking cunt is so hot and wet. I don't think I'll be able to wait much longer."

I shattered, my orgasm quick but strong.

"Holy shit."

I was just as surprised as Dominick. I'd always thought I hated that word, too, but apparently, it was only when referring to women instead of my body part.

"Now, I really can't wait." He lifted my hips and drove inside me.

He felt huge inside me now that I was swollen, and I might have made a noise.

"Did I hurt you?"

"No. Just tender." I grabbed his face and kissed him. "A good tender."

We kissed again, and within minutes I was rotating my hips, urging Dominick to move. He steadily began to thrust, lightly at first, but it wasn't long before he held nothing back.

I clutched at his back as he shoved one of my legs over his shoulder, so he could bury himself even further. It was like he couldn't get deep enough, but I felt the same way. I pulled at him, wanting to feel him everywhere.

Dominick somehow managed to brush the hair out of my face as he continued to move. "Viv, Viv, it's okay."

"More."

"I know; I know. Don't worry. I'm going to make that sweet cunt come."

Then, not as suddenly as the first time, but still a surprise, I exploded again. This orgasm was softer, but it continued on much longer than the previous one. It didn't end until Dominick grabbed my hips one last time and rammed into me as he erupted in pleasure.

He collapsed onto the bed beside me, and that was when I realized we were both covered in sweat.

I put my hand on my chest to feel the racing of my heart. "Oh my God."

Dominick turned his head and smiled at me. "God had nothing to do with that." He rolled over and put his hand over my lower belly. "You know, the first time I said cunt, I did it as a joke, figuring you'd yell at me."

"Did you want me to yell at you?"

He laughed. "Probably not. Maybe. It could have been hot."

"Normally, I'm not a fan, but I guess it works for me in the bedroom. I was as shocked as you."

"I'd say. Now, I have the secret word to get you off. You know what this means, right?"

"No."

He slid his fingers lower, in between my legs, to cup me. "This is mine now."

I laughed and flung his hand away. "In your dreams."

He snatched me around the waist and pulled me close, a cocky grin on his face. "I don't know if there's going to be much dreaming tonight."

"Oh? So, you're not taking me home?"

"Sorry, baby. This appointment is going to take longer than I thought."

EIGHTEEN
VIVIAN

SITTING UP SLOWLY, I MADE SURE NOT TO DISTURB THE sleeping man beside me. But when my muscles and tired brain protested as I stood up, I considered that *man* might be too nice of a term.

Sex addict or *sex fiend* seemed more fitting with the number of times we'd had sex last night.

I looked around for my phone and remembered that it was still in my purse. And my purse was in Dominick's car, where I had left it last night, thinking I was going to hop back inside after we dropped off his brother's car.

I'd make time to get it, but first, I needed to use the bathroom. And wouldn't you know it? I couldn't find my pajamas either, but Dominick's T-shirt was on the floor by the bed.

I yanked it over my head and rushed out into the hall to get to the bathroom. I barely had the door closed before I landed on the toilet and let my bladder go. I sighed with relief and closed my eyes as the pain slowly faded away.

When I was finished, I went to use the toilet paper, only to find the roll empty. This time, I sighed in frustration. Why couldn't men just put a new roll on the empty dispenser? As I searched around, my eyes rounded when I saw the number of condom wrappers in the garbage.

Had we really had that much sex? I'd been half-joking when I called him a sex fiend in my head. My next thought was, I was grateful he'd remembered to use condoms, which was quickly followed by a worry that all of them hadn't been used with me.

That snapped me out of my thoughts, and I continued my hunt and found toilet paper under the sink. As I washed my hands, I reassured myself I was only worried about Dominick having sex with other people because I wanted to make sure he was safe with everyone and not because I was jealous.

Because, of course, someone like Dominick was having sex with more than just one person.

"You need to go. You'll feel better once you're home," I said to my messy-haired reflection.

With a goal to focus on, I decided it was definitely time to wake Dominick up and ask him for a ride as I opened the door to leave the bathroom.

"Oof," I said as I ran into whoever was in the hall on their way to the very place I was leaving.

We both jumped back in shock.

A dark-haired man stared back at me when I finally took a moment to see who I'd crashed into.

"I'm sorry," I said.

He smiled at me, and that was when I realized how young he was. He had to be around seventeen or eighteen, but I could see he was going to be as handsome as Dominick when he was finished growing.

"You must be Dominick's brother," I said.

"I am. And you must be the one who made all that noise last night and the reason there's a mountain of condom wrappers in the bathroom."

Self-conscious, I tugged at the bottom of Dominick's T-shirt. "I wouldn't say a mountain."

A strong arm wrapped around me and pulled me back to an equally strong chest. "Spencer, is that how you speak to guests?" Dominick scolded.

Spencer grinned. "I was only kidding." He waved his right hand because his left was in a sling with a cast peeking out of it. "I'm Spencer."

I waved back, not amused at his jokes. "Vivian."

"Besides, I thought I was a guest," Spencer pointed out.

"You're not a guest. You know where everything is, you help yourself, and we both know you'd live here if Marjorie let you."

Spencer's mouth didn't change, but I saw the humor leave his eyes.

Dominick must have noticed it, too, because he kissed the top of my head. "Are you done in there, Viv?"

"Yeah." I held my hand out to the bathroom. "It's all yours."

Dominick took my hand and led me back to his room, where he shoved me up against the door and kissed me. I let myself enjoy the moment for a second before putting my hands on his chest.

"If you think we're having sex again, you're wrong."

He raised his eyebrows.

"My vagina is not having it. She's too sore."

"Now, she's a vagina? I thought you didn't like that word."

I had to smile at his confusion. "No, it just isn't sexy, which is how I feel right now. Sore vagina, tired Vivian."

He brushed his mouth over mine. "You're killing me because I really, really want to kiss your cunt all better."

I groaned, knowing how good his hot mouth would feel on my tender pussy.

But I needed to get home and do some prep work for a case.

And because I knew I could be easily persuaded, I changed the subject. "Who's Marjorie?"

Dominick curled his lip and pivoted away from me. "My mother."

"You call her by her first name?" I asked as I finally spotted my pajama top and bottoms, which were thankfully right next to each other.

"She's lucky I don't call her Bitch."

Whoa. Scooping up my clothes, I hugged them to my chest.

Despite spending all night with Dominick and having sex on a few occasions, I was reminded of how we really didn't know each other. I'd never heard that tone come out of him.

Last night, I had concluded there was animosity between the two, but this sounded like outright hate. As much as I didn't always see eye to eye with my parents, I still loved and respected them.

The attorney in me wanted to know all the facts, but I convinced myself it wasn't time to pry. "I'm sorry," I said to offer some comfort as I pulled on my clothes. "She must have really hurt you to deserve being called that."

Dominick's head whipped around to face me from where he stood at his closet. He looked me up and down. "You're lucky you're dressed or else I'd fuck you right now, sore pussy or no sore pussy."

I could only stare in shock, seeing as that was the last thing I'd expected to come out of his mouth.

He smiled, his eyes still a little sad. "Everyone always says I shouldn't treat my mother that way. Rarely do I ever get someone who automatically takes my side without an explanation."

I shrugged. "I figure you have a good reason."

"You have your phone on you?"

This man was giving me whiplash with the directions this conversation had taken. "It's in your car."

"Go get it. I'll get dressed and meet you in the living room."

The keys were where Dominick had left them, and I quickly ran outside to the car.

True to his word, he was walking out of his room as I was walking into the house.

He motioned with his hand for me to give him the phone. "Unlock it, please."

I didn't know why I trusted him so much. Maybe it was because of the vulnerability I had seen in his eyes minutes ago, or maybe it was some other reason. Either way, I did as he'd asked.

He typed away, concentration all over his face. He paused a moment to pull out his own phone. He waited for it to buzz and typed something in there. He must have texted himself from my cell.

He checked my phone, nodded when he was satisfied with what he saw, and looked up at me.

"My mom is an alcoholic who won't let me have custody of my sixteen-year-old brother because she likes control and her welfare checks more than the two of us." He handed my phone back to me. "She's also why Spencer broke his arm. I had to take him to the hospital yesterday, which is the only reason he's staying here at the moment. She doesn't want family services called on her."

"Oh, Dominick."

He shook his head. "No feeling sorry for me."

I smiled. "I would never."

"I wouldn't expect anything less."

Dropping my phone back in my purse, I pulled out my

business card. "You know, I might be able to have someone help you with your brother."

He shook his head adamantly. "Absolutely not."

"What?" I dropped my hand, shocked at his reaction. "Why not?"

His eyes narrowed. "I'm not fucking you because you can help me."

His sense of honor only made me like him more.

I touched his arm gently. "I know." I waited until he met my eyes. "I know," I repeated. "But I'm also here if you ever need my help." I slid my card onto the table next to his keys.

"I won't." His face was stern with conviction.

"I know." I smiled reassuringly. "But it's still here...just in case."

NINETEEN
VIVIAN

ONE MONTH LATER

"I don't want to go in there," I said outside the classroom door.

"It's a room full of kids," Rayne said, as if to say it wasn't a big deal.

I held up a finger. "Correction: a room full of high school girls."

Delaney laughed. "You can get up in front of a judge and jury without any problem, but a random high school class has you freaking out?" She tapped her chin. "I might need to rethink my intimidation tactics," she joked.

I shrugged. "I don't understand it either. But I'm comfortable with doing my job. Even if it's a tough case, it becomes a challenge." I pointed toward the door. "This does not feel like a challenge. It feels like I would rather turn around and leave. This makes me uncomfortable."

Rayne put her hand on my shoulder, a sympathetic look on her face. "You weren't bullied in high school, were you? It never even crossed my mind that you might have been."

"Thanks, but, no, I wasn't bullied. I wasn't popular or unpopular. I was just...there." I shrugged again. "Which is why I don't understand this."

Delaney looked at her watch. "Maybe it's because it's something new and unfamiliar. You don't know what to expect."

Huh. I gave it consideration. "You know, you might be right." I liked doing new things at work to push myself to be a better lawyer, but at the same time, it was still my regular job, which gave me comfort. No wonder I'd dated my last boyfriend for so long.

"Don't worry too much," Rayne said. "You have us. You won't be up there alone, and we've been planning this for a month. We are going to do great."

"Rayne's right," Delaney said.

I looked at the two of them. "Okay. I'm trusting you both on this."

"As you should," Rayne said, smiling.

"And if you end up being wrong, I'm just going to sue you."

———

"Does anyone have any more questions?" Delaney asked the class.

We'd already been asked about a dozen questions, so I felt nothing but relief when no one else raised their hand.

The teacher clapped her hands. "We're almost out of time as it is, so let's give a big round of applause for these three, shall we?"

The class clapped, and Rayne, Delaney, and I gave our thanks and our good-byes.

Once the door to the classroom was closed, Rayne elbowed me. "See, that wasn't so bad, was it?"

I smiled. "It was okay."

It hadn't been as bad as I had thought it would be. In fact, I was willing to admit that the forty-five minutes had gone faster than I'd expected, but I was still relieved to be done.

"Is it time for lunch then?" Delaney asked as we headed down the hall.

"Yes, please." Rayne put her hand on her stomach. "Talking to high school students has me starved."

We were almost to the front door of the school when the bell rang.

The three of us looked at each other, and someone yelled, "*Run.*"

Filled with laughter, we raced outside as fast as we could with high heels on our feet, and we exited the building just as the hallways began to fill with students.

"We made it." I raised my fist in the air. "Victory."

Now that we didn't have to worry about being run over by kids rushing to their next class, we strolled to the guest parking area.

"Where's lunch today?" I asked.

"I don't know," Delaney said. "I think it's Rayne's turn to pick a restaurant."

"Hmm..." Rayne rubbed her hands together. "I'm feeling like pizza."

Immediately, Delaney and I exchanged looks. Rayne had been eating nothing but salads since our first lunch together because she was worried about her weight. I hated to see her denying herself food for a man, but it definitely wasn't my place to say anything. We'd only met a month ago, and we weren't close friends.

"Pizza?" I casually said in a way that invited her to tell us more, but it wasn't an outright question if she didn't want to share.

"Yeah. I'm tired of trying to get my boyfriend's attention. If he doesn't think I'm sexy the way I am, then fuck him."

"Good for you," Delaney said.

"I agree. If he doesn't love you the way you are, get rid of him." Although she hadn't exactly said that. "Does this mean you're going to break up with him?"

"No."

Why? was my first thought, but I caught myself before saying it out loud.

"I finally decided it was time to stop guessing what he was thinking and just ask him." Rayne smiled. "Actually, my brother told me to stop assuming and talk to him. So, I did."

"Smart brother," Delaney said.

Rayne smiled. "Well, it was all probably my sister-in-law, secretly telling my brother what to say, so she likely deserves the credit." She waved her hand. "Anyway, I sat my boyfriend down and flat-out asked him if he wasn't attracted to me anymore."

My eyes widened with surprise. I couldn't see her being so bold.

"He actually looked so shocked that I believed him. I'd figured he would deny it and make excuses." She laughed. "But he seemed at a loss for words, and it was honestly the best response."

"But did he give you a reason for why things have been different?" I asked.

"His job has been stressful, and he's been tired."

I called bullshit. That seemed to be every man's excuse. Sure, it could be legitimate. Everyone got tired and overworked sometimes, but it was still suspicious, if you asked me. But since she hadn't, I wasn't going to say anything else.

I did, however, glance over at Delaney, and if I was reading the look on her face correctly, she didn't quite trust the boyfriend's excuse either.

Rayne's expression slowly transformed into pure happiness. "And we're going on vacation for a whole week. Just the two of us. No work, no family, no friends, no commitments but each other." She lifted her shoulders up and beamed. "I'm kind of excited."

"It's always good to get away," Delaney said very diplomatically.

I just hoped for Rayne's sake, her boyfriend was telling the truth.

But I sure was grateful that I was single. The *sex appointment* stuff was working out perfectly for me.

TWENTY

VIVIAN

> D Appointment: You coming over
> tonight? Or am I coming there?

I PUT MY FEET UP ON THE EDGE OF MY DESK AND grinned. When Dominick had put his number into my phone, he had called himself *D Appointment*, and I hadn't bothered to change it.

The truth was, it made me smile every time a message popped up from him.

> Me: I don't recall us having plans.

> D Appointment: We do now.

> Me: Since when? Says who?

> D Appointment: Now. Me.

> D Appointment: I need inside you
> real bad.

Damn. Even with bad grammar, his dirty talk made me hot. So hot that I didn't even correct it.

> Me: What if I told you I actually have
> plans tonight and I can't?

> D Appointment: I'd cry.

Laughing, I sent him another text.

> Me: You would not.

I didn't believe he'd cry for a minute. Not over sex.

> Me: I'm working late.

Dominick sent me back a crying emoji.

I went in search of a GIF of someone rolling their eyes when there was a knock on my doorframe. I sighed when I saw it was Kirk. I didn't want to be working with his incompetent ass on this case, and he had just ruined my good mood.

I pulled my feet to the floor and sat up straight. "Yes?"

"We're going to get takeout for dinner. Do you want in?"

"Yes, please. What restaurant?"

"The sub place."

"Got it. Is someone going to get it, or are we having it delivered?"

If we were really busy, we often got food delivered, but sometimes, one of us needed a break and would pick up dinner.

"I'm making the run," Kirk said. "I'm going in about forty-five minutes or so."

"Okay. I'll put my order in through my phone app."

Kirk disappeared when I was struck with a thought.

"Kirk," I yelled.

Two seconds later, he was back. "Yeah?"

"Is it okay if I go pick up the food?"

His eyebrows squished together. "Uh...sure."

I sprang up from my chair and grabbed my purse. "I have to run a quick errand first, but I'll be back with the food." I looked at my watch. "Tell everyone to have their order ready in an hour," I said as I hurried past Kirk.

"An hour?" he complained.

"Yeah. I need to do something first."

"Are you sure? I can get it."

I spun around and walked backward. "I said, I'll get it."

"Fine."

I did another one-eighty and unlocked my phone.

Me: Where are you right now?

D Appointment: My backyard. Why?

He was going to have to wait for the answer to that because he wasn't the only one who was horny.

I walked around the house. Rock music blared from the backyard, and the fence door was wide open. I walked through it and slammed it closed behind me.

The sound was loud enough for Dominick to turn around. He was shirtless and covered in sweat that ran down to his low shorts, making his skin glisten under the setting sun.

He had a bundle of sticks in his hands, as if he were in the process of moving them. But when he saw me, he dropped them and tore his work gloves off his hands. We met halfway, and despite the fact that I was wearing a nice blouse and dressy skirt, I launched myself at him.

I kissed him as his hot, sweaty hands went under my skirt and squeezed my ass. He walked backward as I moaned into his mouth.

"I thought you had plans tonight?" he asked.

"I do. I only have about fifteen minutes. We have to make this fast." I glanced over his shoulder to see we had reached the steps to his deck, so I pushed him down.

He landed on his ass with a thud that made him laugh. But his smile turned to pure lust when I lifted my skirt and slid my underwear off.

He sucked on his bottom lip and scraped his teeth over it. "Fuck yes, but, Viv, I had no idea you were coming. I don't have a condom."

I reached into my shirt and slipped two fingers under the cup of my bra to pull out the condom I had stashed there. I threw it at him and said, "You'd better hurry, or I'm going to come without you."

"Yeah, right."

He had the rubber on before I could blink twice, and he snagged me around the waist and yanked me over to him. I grabbed his cock and placed it at my entrance, and then I dropped my weight onto him as I wrapped my hands around his neck.

Dominick swore so loudly that his neighbors probably heard it over his music. But I used the pounding beat to let out a long moan as he filled me. I could feel his dick everywhere, and I started rotating my hips until I was riding him toward an orgasm.

My shirt was whipped open and my bra pulled down as Dominick seized one breast to bring to his mouth. He sucked hard, and I moaned again as I dug my claws into his head.

Somehow, I managed to ride him harder, and it wasn't long until my climax was just over the horizon. I just needed one more push, which, after a month of us sleeping together, Dominick seemed to sense.

He bit down on my hard tip as he slapped my ass, and I shattered as waves of pleasure crashed over me. I came so hard that my pussy tightened around Dominick's length to the point of almost pain, and he released my nipple and groaned into my neck.

I floated as if in a dream for a minute or two until my senses slowly evened out and I felt like my limbs might work again. Below, I still throbbed in tiny aftershocks of pleasure.

Dominick's head was resting between my breasts while my upper half was draped over him like a rag doll. His still-hard cock twitched inside me, and I loved knowing I'd made him come too. As a thank-you and a you're-welcome, I squeezed my inner muscles around his shaft.

He lifted his head from my chest and gently kissed me. "You do that again, and I don't care what kind of plans you have; I'm taking you inside and fucking you all... night...long."

TWENTY-ONE
VIVIAN

I GROANED BUT SLOWLY LIFTED MYSELF OFF OF HIM and pulled down my skirt. I only now thought about his neighbors possibly being able to see us from a window. I also noticed the music had stopped. *When did that happen?*

Dominick made quick work of the condom and flipped his workout shorts back over his semi-hard-on. He leaned back on his elbows and grinned up at me.

"Why are you smiling at me?"

"A guy can't smile at the woman who just fucked his brains out?"

"Yes, but you look too cocky."

He opened a hand, and my underwear dropped from his fist to hang from one finger. He leaned forward. "You almost forgot these."

I reached for them, but Dominick yanked them out of my grasp.

"Dominick," I tried to say with some authority. "I need those."

He tilted his head and studied the top of my skirt to the bottom. He sat back up. "No, you don't. Your skirt is almost to your knees." He waved his hand in a gentle sway. "Your panties are staying with me tonight."

I shoved my hands onto my hips. "You can't keep my underwear."

"Sure I can. They smell like your cunt, and I want them."

My pussy clenched, and wetness flooded my core. How I was turned on again so quickly, I didn't know. But it was proof that I needed my panties back.

I lost all traces of a smile and held out my hand. "I'm serious. I need them. And I need them now because I have to pick up food for my coworkers and get back to the firm."

Dominick jumped up from the stairs and put his arm around my shoulders. "Okay, okay, okay. I understand. Let me walk you to your car."

"What happened to the music?" I asked as he walked me to the front of the house.

"I turned it off." He smiled. "My phone is in my pocket."

"You waited until we were finished, right?"

"Oh, yeah. I didn't need the neighbors hearing you moan like it was the second coming of Christ."

My mouth dropped open. "I don't moan," I lied. "I don't make noise, remember?"

He bopped me on the nose with a finger from his free

hand. "Whatever you have to tell yourself, babe." We reached my car, and he opened the driver's door for me. "Your chariot awaits, milady."

I looked him up and down in fake judgment. "You would not have fit in back then."

He laughed. "Why? Because of my unruly curls? Because of my facial hair?" He snapped his fingers. "Or is it because I'm Cuban?"

"No, it's because you only think about sex."

He laughed and moved close. "Only around you, babe."

Yeah, right. This man lived and breathed sex.

"Speaking of sex"—I had almost forgotten—"what are you doing on Saturday night? Are you free to meet up?"

I had to have dinner with my parents on Saturday. And while I loved them, they were always a lot to put up with. Especially when I was the only child of theirs around to bother. I knew I could use some good sex after seeing them.

He rubbed his beard and hissed in what sounded like regret, and I had a feeling about what he was going to say. "I can't. I'm busy."

I smiled. "It's okay. I understand. It is less than a week away. I can't expect a stud like you to be free on a Saturday night."

He rolled his eyes, but I saw the smile threatening to break free. "You'd better get going." He nudged me toward the open door. "I don't want you to get in trouble."

"Wait." I frowned.

"What?"

I studied his face. I felt like I was missing something, but I couldn't figure out what. "Never mind," I said when nothing came to mind.

He kissed me, and I slid behind the wheel.

"Call me if your night ends early."

"I will, but it won't." I turned the key, and when the clock turned on, I gasped. "Shit, I need to go." I waved good-bye, slammed my door closed, and raced to the restaurant.

Thankfully, we were only getting cold sandwiches, but I still didn't need anyone looking at me and wondering why I was so late.

I was only five minutes behind the time I had scheduled the pickup. I hurried back to my vehicle with the food and into the building as soon as my car was safely parked.

When I was almost to the conference room, I slowed my pace and put a casual smile on my face. "Food's here," I called out as I walked through the door.

I dumped the bags out on the counter, and everyone dived toward their food. I found my sub and an open chair.

I set my food down and turned to go back to my office to get my computer when one of my colleagues, another associate named Faren, said, "Oh my God. What happened to you?"

My eyes rounded. "What?" I asked, my heart racing. In the car, I had finger-combed my hair at stoplights. And I had made sure what was left of my makeup wasn't smeared on my face.

"Your blouse. It has buttons missing," she said.

I looked down to see that my shirt was hanging open and the top of my bra was showing. "I got caught on my car door. I didn't even notice; I was in such a hurry," I lied. "I have another shirt in my office."

I always had at least one backup in case I spilled coffee or food on myself.

Or if the guy I was hooking up with ripped the buttons off.

"I'll be right back," I muttered as I grabbed my phone before heading down the hall.

> Me: Thanks for sending me back to work like this.

I hoped he could hear my sarcasm all the way from my office building.

> D Appointment: I told you I was keeping your panties.

Shocked, I stopped in my tracks and patted my butt. "That asshole," I muttered.

> D Appointment: Don't worry. I'll make sure nothing bad happens to them while you're away.

> D Appointment: But if you want them back, you're going to have to come and get them.

I couldn't believe he had distracted me to the point that

I hadn't noticed I didn't have any underwear on at my place of employment.

Me: I hate you.

D Appointment: That's okay, babe, because you love my dick.

I couldn't stop the smile that came over my face. He was ridiculous and sexy and even cute sometimes. Like now. But it was a good thing he was just a guy I had sex with because we were too different...even though I could really see myself falling for him.

TWENTY-TWO
VIVIAN

"AND THEN THE KID WAS LATE AGAIN." MY FATHER shrugged. "So, I fired him."

"Wow," I said with little enthusiasm.

My dad seemed to think I liked hearing about his job. Or maybe it was because we didn't have much in common, so we didn't have many things to talk about.

"How's your work, Vivian?" my mom asked.

"Going well. I'm doing this program with the Minneapolis mayor's office. It's not for the firm, but it should be beneficial for my career."

Both my parents beamed.

"Honey, why didn't you tell us?" Mom asked.

I couldn't help but smile at their joy. "I don't know. It's not really my thing, but I know it will look good on my résumé."

"What is it you're doing?" Dad asked.

I explained what Women in Law was and how we

were going around to schools to encourage young girls to pursue a career in law.

"Hmm," Dad said. "Why lawyers?"

I knew my father was just asking out of curiosity, but I couldn't help but feel like it was a slight toward my career choice.

"Probably because the mayor's an attorney," I explained, no longer feeling as proud of myself as I had a minute ago.

I picked up my napkin from my lap and set it on my plate, and then I looked around for our server. My parents had picked a chain bar and grill. More and more people were starting to come through the door, and soon, the place was going to be full. We were off in one corner of the restaurant, and it had been peaceful since we'd arrived early, but it wouldn't be for long. I was ready to call it a night.

While I hoped our server would be the next person to come around the corner, I watched the door to the restaurant open, and then Dominick walked in.

I looked to my parents and back to Dominick. I didn't know what to do. *Should I introduce him? What would my parents think? They've probably never pictured me with a guy covered in tattoos. Would it cause a problem between us?* Or maybe it didn't matter because Dominick would just be introduced as a friend. They would probably still disapprove, but they wouldn't be worried about me dating him. Which, technically, I wasn't anyway, but they definitely wouldn't approve of me sleeping with someone outside of a relationship.

As I contemplated what to do, I had to blink a couple of times to see if my eyes were playing tricks on me, but they weren't.

Gina had just walked in behind Dominick. She said something, and they both cracked up as they approached the hostess stand. And while he didn't have his arm around her, they were standing very close.

White-hot jealousy coursed through me along with a sinking feeling in my abdomen. It was fortunate I had finished eating because I lost my appetite, and what food I had consumed felt like rocks in my stomach now.

"Vivian. *Vivian*."

I turned back to my parents and saw a look of concern on my mom's face.

"Honey, are you okay?"

No. Everything was wrong. I hadn't realized how much I'd wanted to introduce him to my parents until I found out I couldn't.

I grabbed my purse. "Actually, I really don't feel well." I pulled out my wallet and put some cash on the table. "Is it okay if I head out without you?"

My dad picked up the money and handed it back to me. "Your mother and I are paying for this. You just go."

"Are you sure?"

"Yes," they both said.

I wasn't in the mood to argue about who was going to pay tonight.

Without putting the cash back in my wallet, I shoved everything back in my purse. "Thank you."

"Wow. She really doesn't feel good if she's not going to fight us about paying," Mom said.

I had to smile at this, but it was short-lived as I waited for Dominick and Gina to be seated soon. I just hoped it wouldn't be in our section.

Panic came over me as I realized that I would have no idea what to say if I came face-to-face with the two of them together. Acting normal would be my goal, but I didn't know if I could manage that when I felt like I was going to throw up.

Thankfully, the hostess went a different way, and the two of them disappeared from my sight. And that was my cue to leave.

"Thanks, Mom. Thanks, Dad."

"You're welcome, honey," my mom said while I walked away.

I felt rude for not hugging her good-bye, but I needed to get out of the building. I rushed out as fast as I could without running because that would only draw more attention to myself, but I didn't watch where I was going, and I ran into someone on my way out.

"Oof."

I looked up to see a big guy with a blond buzz cut. For some reason, he looked vaguely familiar, but I didn't have time to think about that.

"Sorry," I muttered and hurried away.

It wasn't until I was in my car with the door closed that I felt like I could breathe normally.

After a couple of deep breaths, I started my vehicle and headed home.

Seeing Dominick had been a wake-up call for me. The whole reason I had wanted a D appointment was because I didn't want to be in a relationship. And here I was, getting jealous over the guy I was having sex with.

The worst part was, it had snuck up on me. I hadn't even realized I was catching feelings for him until I saw him with Gina.

I moaned at the recent memory.

Truth be told, I was mad. I wasn't mad at Dominick. He and I were not in a relationship. He had never committed himself to me, and he had every right to be with whoever he wanted to be with. I was mad at myself.

But why Gina?

I straightened my spine.

Nope.

"No, no, no, no, no, no," I said to myself out loud. "Knock it off."

Gina had probably hooked me up with Dominick because she knew he was good in bed. I didn't think that was something I could ever do—have sex with someone and then hook them up with another person—but I wasn't her, and I needed to let it go.

Dominick wasn't mine. I had no right to feel territorial. And I needed to get over it.

I needed to end the *sex arrangement* thing we had going on before my feelings got worse.

My first instinct was to grab my phone and text him right away to tell him we were done, but I stopped myself. Not only was I driving, but also, if I did it out of nowhere, it was going to look suspicious. He was going to know something was up. And I absolutely *did not* want him to know I had seen him tonight. I didn't need humiliation added on to jealousy and the little touch of heartbreak I was feeling.

I would just tell him no the next time he messaged me.

If only I could not think about it until then. I needed a distraction.

My sister was a quick contact on my car's display, and I hit the Call button.

"Hey, what's up?" Kat said when she answered.

"I just had dinner with Mom and Dad."

She groaned and laughed. She was the diversion I needed.

It turned out, I didn't have to wait long for Dominick to text me.

The next morning, after I cleaned my whole apartment, he messaged me.

> D Appointment: How was your night?
> Did you miss me?

"Probably not as fun as yours," I said in a snotty tone.

> Me: It was fine. I had dinner with my parents.

I didn't answer the "miss me" question.

> D Appointment: I've been lying here, thinking about you.

"You didn't have enough sex last night? Jeez."

I dropped my arm and used my free hand to rub my forehead.

I was not being fair to Dominick. I was letting my anger with myself be rude to him. I hated that I had to remind myself that he had done nothing wrong. I was the one who had caught feelings.

> Me: I'm sorry, Dominick, but I think we need to end this thing we have going on. I recently took on more cases at my work, and while it's been really fun, I can't be distracted anymore.

My thumb hovered over the Send button. "Ah," I yelled out and hit it.

> D Appointment: Shit, babe, that came out of nowhere.

I closed my eyes and willed myself not to cry. It was the "babe." Somewhere in the last month, he'd started calling me that, and even though my rational brain had known he probably called a lot of women the same thing, my irrational brain had thought I was special.

D Appointment: You wound me.

I barked out a laugh. "Please don't be sweet and funny," I begged even though he couldn't hear me.

Me: Please don't be. You are great. Your dick is great. The sex is great. I just don't have time for sex anymore. Not right now.

D Appointment: You're great too, babe. Hit me up if you need me again.

Me: I will.

But I knew that I definitely wouldn't.

TWENTY-THREE
DOMINICK

I leaned against the hood of my car as I watched the woman from family services come out of my mom's trailer and head for her vehicle.

That's it?

"Wait," I yelled as I ran over to her. "You're not going to take Spencer with you?"

She sighed, but it wasn't out of disappointment or sadness. It was out of irritation. She held up a hand. "Sir, this doesn't concern you."

"Like hell it doesn't. That's my brother in there," I said, pointing to the trailer home. "He deserves better." I deserved better.

A look of sympathy finally passed over her face. "You're right. He does. But there is food in the fridge, your brother is clean, and he has clothes on his back." She stepped around me. "I'm sorry. There's nothing more I can do."

I spun around and watched helplessly as she got in her car and drove away. I kicked the dirt under my feet and yelled, "*Goddammit.*"

When Spencer had called me that family services was here because someone at the hospital had made a complaint, I had gotten my hopes up way too high. If I had known she was coming, I wouldn't have bought groceries for my brother yesterday even though I knew that was only part of it.

The screen door squeaked, and Marjorie stepped out. "What are you yelling about out here?"

My bitch of a mother had all the luck. Today, she had showered and put on makeup because her loser boyfriend was taking her to the casino. It was also why she wasn't as drunk as she normally was.

If only the social worker had come yesterday.

"Nothing," I said, finally answering her despite her knowing exactly why I was pissed.

"Good. Then, can you get your stupid car out of the way, so we can leave?"

"Send Spencer out here, and I'll do just that."

"Spence," she yelled over her shoulder. Then, she turned back to me and pointed a finger. "You're not taking him anywhere. He'd better be here when I get back home."

"Yeah, yeah, I fucking know."

She laughed and moved out of the way for Spencer to come out.

"Hey," he said as he jogged over.

"What did the social worker say?"

Spencer shrugged. "Not much. The usual."

I knew how that went. They poked around, asked questions right in front of our mother, and then left.

"I'm sorry," I said.

He shrugged again. "It's not your fault."

"Did you say anything?"

He kicked a pebble on the ground. "No."

I didn't understand why Spencer didn't do more to be taken away. I had never heard him defend Marjorie, but he didn't complain about her either. When he had been little, I'd thought it was because he was worried she'd beat him, but he was bigger than her now. The *broken arm* thing was kind of a fluke. If Spencer went toe-to-toe with our mother, he'd win. I never understood why he held back when someone who could help him arrived, and whenever I asked, he wouldn't give me a straight answer.

Not wanting him to feel guilty, I rubbed the hair on his head and asked, "How's the arm?"

"Good." Smiling, he lifted his cast. "Look at all the signatures I have on it." He pointed to one in pink. "Even the most popular girl in school signed it."

I laughed. "You're such a stud."

"Shut up, Dom."

"Listen, I need to go, but if you need anything, call me."

He nodded. "Okay."

"And, hey, at least you'll be by yourself tonight."

"Yeah."

"Later, bro."

"Later."

I hopped in my car and took off. Not in the mood to go home, I headed to Tony's house just so I wouldn't sit and think about my brother.

And so I wouldn't text Vivian.

When she had told me she needed to cut things off with me, it had come as a surprise. A few days earlier, she had asked if I was free on Saturday night, and then Sunday, she was suddenly too busy?

It didn't feel right, but I didn't push. I had agreed to be her D appointment, and if she needed a break, I was going to give her time.

But it had made me wonder what would have happened if I had canceled my plans with Tony and Gina and gone over to Vivian's instead.

Speaking of my two friends, I knocked on Tony's front door and opened it before I got an answer because Tony and I had known each other for years. I found the two of them snuggling on the couch.

"Hey, man," Tony said when he saw it was me.

"Hey. I'm not interrupting anything, am I?"

"We're just watching some TV until dinner is done."

"Hey, Dom," Gina said.

"Hey." I sniffed the air as I sat down on the adjacent recliner. "Smells good."

Tony grinned. "I cooked."

I raised my eyebrows. "What the fuck?"

He laughed. "I know."

Gina sat up. "He's pretty good at it too."

"I'm good at a lot of things," Tony said to her.

I made a gagging sound.

I couldn't believe that these two hadn't even known each other until I introduced them. When Tony had told me he was taking Gina on a date, I had secretly laughed. Now, they were together all the time.

Tony whipped his head around. "No one invited you, dude," he joked. And because he knew me so well, he asked, "Bad day?"

I ran my hand over my hair. "Yeah. Family services came and didn't do jack shit."

"I'm sorry, Dom," Gina said. "I had such high hopes..."

I frowned. "What are you talking about? You didn't know they were showing up at my mom's today."

She looked away. "I just meant that I had high hopes you'd be able to get your brother soon."

It almost felt like she was lying, but I didn't know about what. Gina had been very supportive of me getting custody of Spencer and never seemed to fake her concern. But I was probably just hyperaware of any little nuance.

"Yeah, man, sorry to hear that," Tony said.

I sighed, rested my head back on the chair, and closed my eyes. "Just a couple more years, and he'll be eighteen, and then I won't have to deal with this shit anymore."

After a minute, when neither of them had responded, I opened my eyes and looked over at them. They were looking at each other like they were ridiculously in love.

This was the whole reason I wished I had skipped the concert. I had felt like the third wheel all night. And I had missed out on getting naked with Vivian.

"How's work going?" I asked.

Tony looked at me like I was nuts. "Same shit, different day."

"Not you. Gina."

"Fine," she said with a shrug. "I sure wish you were still screwing Vivian though."

"Oh?" I said casually. And I'd thought I was going to have to pry information out of Gina.

"Yeah, she's passed Suzie Stern and gone to Betty Bitch. No one wants to be around her."

I was sure Gina had to be exaggerating, but I didn't interrupt.

"She bit my head off the other day, and then she had the nerve to ask me to hook her up with someone. Or rather, she *almost* asked me to hook her up with someone. She only hinted, and once I brought up your name, she told me she changed her mind and rushed out of there." Gina shook her head. "She needs to get her shit together."

I was leaning forward, arms on my legs by this point. "What do you mean, she asked you to hook her up with someone?" I needed Gina to repeat what she had told me.

"She said something like she really needed a D appointment. I knew you two had taken a break, so I offered to text you, but she booked it back to her office. It wasn't until she left that I wondered if she wanted to hook up with a different guy." Her nose wrinkled. "Did something bad happen between the two of you?"

I was at the door before Gina finished her sentence because I was going to find out why the fuck Vivian had lied to me.

TWENTY-FOUR
VIVIAN

I rubbed my neck as I walked down the hall to my apartment, trying to relieve the stress that had built up there.

Things were so bad that, yesterday, I had almost asked Gina if she could hook me up with another one of her friends.

That was how desperate I was.

But as soon as she'd mentioned Dominick, I had known it was a bad idea. I couldn't tell her why he was no longer an option, and did I really want to go with another guy that Gina recommended to me? Was that really the smart choice? Probably not.

Especially when what I really wanted was him.

So, it was best to stay away from all men right now. At least until I shed some of these unwanted feelings.

But the fact that I had them confirmed that I was doing the right thing.

If only I could make myself delete his number from my Contacts list.

So, rather than asking Gina for another hookup, I had signed up for a kickboxing class. Tonight was the first night I'd done it, and while it hadn't done anything to relieve my tension, I was tired. Hopefully, I would have a dreamless night.

I reached my door, and just as I turned the lock, a shadow fell over me.

I gasped. "What are you doing here?"

"You lied to me," Dominick said and pushed open my door and me inside.

"I didn't lie," I said as he shoved me against the wall.

My apartment was dark, but the streetlights put off enough of a glow for me to see his grim expression. He was pissed.

"Now, you're lying about lying." His hand went around my neck, and he pressed his body flush against mine. "I told you not to lie to me."

He tightened his hand.

"I came here to ask you why." His eyes roamed my face. "But all I can do is think about fucking your sweet cunt."

He'd said the secret word on purpose. It had to have been on purpose.

Even if it wasn't, it had the same effect on me, and I drew in a shaky breath.

I wanted him to fuck me too.

We'd slept together enough times for Dominick to

know my body language, and his mouth came crashing down on mine. The second our lips connected, it was as if something inside of me took over.

I ripped at his clothes and my own, wanting to feel his bare skin on mine. I didn't know who undressed who, but moments later, I was naked, and Dominick lifted me up against the wall.

My thighs were already coated with my desire, and all I was missing was him. With one move, he slammed into me, and I immediately came. I clawed at Dominick's back as he rode me through my orgasm as if he couldn't get enough of me.

Even though I had come, I held him tight. I didn't want him to leave. I wanted him to stay inside me forever.

It wasn't long before we were both covered in sweat, and my back was getting sore from the wall, but I didn't care. I opened my legs wider, as if to keep him there.

His breathing quickened, and so did my own. With each thrust, I was brought closer to exploding again.

"*Oh God,*" I cried out as my second climax tore through my body.

"Fuck," he yelled. "I can't—" He groaned long and low as he drove into me one last time and jerked inside me. "Goddammit. You feel too good."

Our combined breathing was the only sound in the apartment as he slowly set me on my feet without backing away.

"You told me you would still come to me if you needed

me. But I know you asked Gina about fucking someone else."

"I—"

"Save it," he bit out. "If you were done with me, you should have just said so. You didn't need to lie."

He stepped back and scanned my naked body as he buttoned up his pants.

I wanted to reach out to him, but I didn't know what to say. I didn't know how to explain how I felt.

He shook his head, as if he sensed my urge to touch him. "The good news is, you don't have to tell me we're done. I'm telling you instead."

I drew in a sharp breath, and Dominick bent down and picked up his shirt.

When he reached the door, he said, "Do me a favor and lose my number."

That was the last thing he said before he yanked on his shirt and walked out the door.

The slam reverberated through my apartment as I tried not to cry.

But I would not let myself. I was a strong, independent woman, and I wouldn't let myself cry over a man. I hadn't cried when my ex and I broke up, and I wouldn't do it now.

I straightened my spine. I needed a shower and a clean outfit. Washing his scent off of me would help.

I bent over to pick up my clothes from the floor, and a wetness trickled out of me. I rushed over to the light switch, flicked it on, and put my hand between my legs.

My fear was confirmed when I saw Dominick's cum on my fingertips.

He had always used a condom. Always.

Except for tonight.

What a way to say our final good-bye.

It was almost as if he had left with one final *fuck you* to me. I was on birth control, but I didn't know how many people he was sleeping with. And how many people they were sleeping with.

With a sigh, I slowly made my way to my bathroom and turned on the shower, knowing it wasn't going to help much.

Dominick had taken my heart and left his seed inside of me.

TWENTY-FIVE
VIVIAN

TWO MONTHS LATER

"We find the defendant..."

I crossed my fingers as I waited for the jury foreperson to read the verdict. I swore they purposely paused to finish the sentence like we were on some TV show or something.

"Not guilty."

The breath of relief I let out almost made me light-headed. I'd really had no idea which way this case was going to go.

The defendant—Mrs. Lola Vale, a sixty-two-year-old grandma—gave me and Mr. St. James hugs, then went off to hug her family.

"Good job, Vivian."

"Thank you, Mr. St. James." I couldn't help but feel a little bit of pride. I had worked my butt off on this case, and a name partner was here to see it.

He put his notebook in his briefcase. "I think it's time you call me Preston, don't you?"

I didn't think I was ever going to stop smiling. "Thank you, Preston."

"You did good work," he said with a nod and excused himself.

I walked out of the courthouse, feeling like everything I had been working for was becoming worth the sacrifices I'd made.

I was getting used to speaking in front of students with the Women in Law program, and Mrs. Vale had come to Benowitz & St. James, asking for me, because I had spoken at her granddaughter's school. And when Mr. St. James—Preston—had told me he was going to sit second chair to me, I had been floored. It wasn't a big case, and I didn't think it warranted a name partner, but he did it anyway. And it had been worth it because he was there to witness me winning today.

Honestly, Mrs. Vale's case couldn't have come at a better time. She had walked into the firm two days after my last encounter with Dominick. It was the distraction I needed, especially while I waited for my test results and period to arrive. Thankfully, all was good there, and I had been officially man-free since then. I took a lot of kickboxing classes, but I did them by myself. I still missed sex—a lot—but at least my heart wasn't affected adversely.

My phone buzzed in my purse.

Delaney: How did it go today?

Me: We won!

Delaney: I knew you could do it.

Rayne: Congratulations! Celebration drinks later this week?

Me: Yes, please. I need it.

I turned off my screen, feeling guilty that Delaney had been such a great cheerleader and I still hadn't told her where I worked. How it hadn't come up yet, I didn't know. And since she didn't know where I worked, I certainly hadn't told her who I had been sitting next to in court during the last week. I felt like an awful friend, but since that was the worst thing going on in my personal life, I considered myself all good.

If only I could stop the occasional thoughts of Dominick, I'd be perfect.

Slowly, I was pulled from a deep sleep, but I didn't have much time to assess the situation because my phone was ringing.

"Hello?" My voice was rough. I cleared my throat. "This is Vivian."

"Vivian Stern?" a male voice I didn't recognize asked. "The attorney?"

By now, most of the sleep was wearing off, and I saw

that it was after two in the morning. I pulled my phone away. I didn't recognize the number.

"Yes. This is Vivian Stern."

"This is the Minneapolis Police Department. I have your client down here, and he won't talk to us without you."

"What?" I jumped off my bed and looked around for the nearest clothes. "Who did you say is in custody?"

I looked at my cell again, only to see that the call had ended.

"What the fuck?" I yelled.

There had been no introduction, and they hadn't even told me who I was going to see.

As I raced to get dressed, my high-on-life moment around twelve hours earlier seemed like a distant memory.

Getting into a room to see clients was always a process. Right out of law school and fresh from taking the bar exam, I'd worked for the public defender's office. I had been to the police department more times than I could count, so even though it had been a while, I remembered all the steps.

"This way, Ms. Stern," an officer said and headed down the hall.

I had been racking my brain since I'd left my apartment, wondering who could have called me down there. I wasn't working on any criminal cases at the moment, so I had absolutely no idea who was going to be on the other side.

"He's in here," the officer said with a bored expression on his face and opened the door.

Two men in plain clothes were standing against the wall. They had to be detectives. And my client had his back to me, so I could only see his dark brown hair over broad shoulders. It was the last person I'd have imagined would call me down to the police station.

I stepped into the room to face the detectives, going into full lawyer mode.

"Spencer Reyes, don't say another word. Detectives, what is my client being charged with?"

The younger detective looked down at his notepad. "Vandalism, arson, and attempted murder or, depending on what happens to his mother, murder."

Shit.

"I'd like some time alone to speak to my client."

The detectives shuffled out, and I sat across from Spencer.

Once the door was closed and the light to the camera in the corner turned off, I said, "What the hell happened? Why did you call me? Why isn't Dominick here? And this last question is the most important. Did you say *anything* to the police?"

TWENTY-SIX
DOMINICK

It was five in the morning, and I was getting ready to leave for work soon when there was a knock at my front door.

It was still dark outside, and I didn't know a single soul who would be at my doorstep this early in the morning.

I grabbed the bat I kept in the closet just as a precaution and opened the door.

"Please tell me you have coffee," a tired-looking Vivian said as she pushed me out of the way on her way to my kitchen.

Stunned, I stood there with the front door halfway open and my jaw on the floor. The sound of a cupboard door slamming jolted me out of my stupor, and I shut the door, put down the bat, and headed to the kitchen.

Vivian lowered an empty glass from her mouth and gestured it toward me. "Sorry, I needed water first."

"Vivian, what the hell are you doing here?"

When I'd told her I wanted her to lose my number, I'd meant it. But only until the phone buzzed and I found myself hoping it was her. At least for a week or so. I'd come to the conclusion a while ago that she wasn't going to contact me again.

Unfazed by the lack of a greeting, she opened another cupboard door and took out a coffee mug. She poured herself a cup and slowly turned around to face me.

Even with her flat hair, puffy eyes, and wrinkled clothes, I wanted her just as much as I had the last time I saw her.

And then it hit me.

"I need to sit down." But instead of sitting, I fell back against the wall.

It wasn't until after I'd left Vivian's apartment the night I confronted her that I realized I hadn't used a condom. I had told myself it was one time and everything was going to be fine.

But now, she was here to tell me she was pregnant.

"Oh fuck. I'm not ready to be a father." I met her eyes. "But whatever you need from me, it's yours."

"What?" Vivian's brow furrowed in confusion. "No. I got my period; plus, I'm on the pill. Thanks for checking, by the way."

I gulped in a breath of air. *Fuck.* That was close. And I felt like an asshole because she had a point.

"I'm not here because of a kid." She paused and tilted her head back and forth. "Well, not that kid anyway. I'm here about your brother."

"My brother? Whatever for?"

Vivian came over to me and put her hand on my arm. "Dominick, I think you should sit down for this."

"So, my mother is in the hospital, my brother is in juvie, Marjorie's trailer is toast, and my brother is the one accused of setting it on fire," I said, pacing back and forth in my kitchen.

Vivian nodded. "Yes."

"Fuck." I threw my hands up. "I don't even know what to do."

"I know you hate me right now, but will you please let me help? At least for your brother's sake."

"I don't hate you, Vivian. I was just really mad that day. I'm sorry I came over like that. I wasn't intending to fuck you like I did. I've never forgotten a condom before either. I wasn't trying to scare you or prove anything, I swear."

She smiled sympathetically. "I understand. And if I had wanted you to stop, I would have told you to. Calzone, remember?"

I snorted.

"But I'm on birth control, and I went and got tested. Everything is fine."

I frowned. "Tested?"

She laughed as if I didn't get the joke. "Dominick, I don't know who or how many people you've been with."

Is she serious?

She waved a hand back and forth. "But that's not important right now. Immediately, we need to figure out what to do about your brother."

"What do you suggest?"

"Since your mother is in the hospital, we should get an emergency hearing in front of a judge for you to be able to take temporary custody. Then, we get your brother out of juvie on bond at least. Last, we clear his name."

I nodded slowly. "Okay." Suddenly, a thought came to me. "But what if he did it?"

She sighed.

I pointed at her. "You know."

"I can't tell you anything, Dominick, but ask yourself if you think he did it. I think you can go with your gut on this. And once we get him into your custody, you'll be able to speak to him freely."

"I can't go down to juvie and talk to him now?"

"Absolutely not. Everything is recorded. There is no expectation of privacy between brothers."

"Even if you're there?"

"I'm not going to be his lawyer."

"Why not?" I tilted my head. "How did he know to call you anyway?"

"He heard us talking and knew I'd left my card. He memorized my phone number. Smart kid."

I couldn't help but smile. "Yeah, he is." My face went serious. "That doesn't tell me why you can't be his lawyer."

"You want someone with more experience than me.

He's looking at attempted murder or murder if your mother doesn't make it."

I never thought I would wish Marjorie would stay alive so hard.

"And it's a conflict of interest."

"Because you and I used to fuck?"

"Yes, that and…" She shook her head. "Just trust me. It wouldn't work out."

"But I want you to do it."

She stepped forward and took my hand. "If you want me to help, I will. But I'd rather do it as your friend. And as your friend, I'm telling you, he needs a lawyer with more experience in these charges."

I studied her face. Her expression was serious and almost a little afraid, as if she was worried I'd tell her no.

She didn't need to worry.

"You got yourself a deal."

"We'll go to my firm today, and I will find someone to help your brother with his criminal case and someone to help you get custody of Spencer since your mom is in the hospital. Do you think you'll be visiting her today?"

"I'd rather not."

"Think about it. If she doesn't make it, you might regret not saying good-bye."

Footsteps sounded behind us, and Vivian and I both turned to see Gina walking into the kitchen as she rubbed her eyes.

"What are you still doing home, Dom? Don't you need

to get to work?" She dropped her arms and blinked at Vivian. "What are you doing here so early?"

Vivian immediately let go of my hand and stepped back as all the color drained from her face. "Oh." She tried to smile, but it was fake and weak. "I didn't realize you were here." Her eyes darted around, as if she didn't know what to do, before finally meeting mine. "I'll see myself out."

She set down the coffee mug and fled.

"What's her problem?" Gina said.

TWENTY-SEVEN
VIVIAN

I raced toward the front door. My car wasn't close enough.

"Vivian," Dominick called.

Shit, shit, shit. His brother.

I slowed my pace but didn't stop. "I have to go home and shower," I called over my shoulder in a surprisingly steady voice. "Just call me when you're ready." *Or better yet...*"Or Gina can bring you down to the firm later."

I resumed my previous speed and didn't wait for him to answer. I had to get out of there as fast as I could, before I did something embarrassing, like cry.

Thankfully, I made it to my car, got it started without any problems, and zoomed out of the driveway and down the street to go home.

I couldn't believe it. After all this time, I still had feelings for Dominick. And when he'd asked for my help, I'd foolishly believed he had feelings for me too.

And everything had been going so well until last night.

But I couldn't blame Spencer. He had done the right thing, calling me. Or having the police call me. He was in big trouble, and he needed help to get out of it.

He had explained to me that he'd been mad at his mother, so he and a friend spray-painted her car. So, he'd admitted to me about the vandalism, but he'd sworn he didn't start the fire that burned down his mom's trailer.

After he and his friend had tagged the car, they left and went to the friend's house. When he got back home, he discovered the fire. He was the one who called 911, but it seemed like the cops had seen a poor kid and assumed he was guilty. They didn't even have any evidence, just assumptions. And my fear was that if he admitted to the spray-painting, they wouldn't believe he hadn't had anything to do with the fire.

The whole thing was a mess, and the lawyer in me was ready to go to bat for the kid, but I thought that a part of me wanted to help because of Dominick. And that was not a good way to go into a case. The client came first. If I was going to help him, I would need to think about Spencer more than his older brother, which was why I'd told Dominick I couldn't be Spencer's lawyer.

And now, I was thankful I had told him that before I saw Gina. I would still help Dominick, but if I wasn't anyone's lawyer, I could take a step back and separate myself. Because it was going to be hard to be around him so much.

The minute he had opened the door this morning,

everything I'd thought I had gotten over was back. And with his brother and mom situation, I had wanted to throw my arms around him and hug him tight.

I wanted to feel his body close to mine again for more than just comfort.

"You're ridiculous," I told myself as I skipped the elevator and used the stairs to get up to my floor instead.

Once in my apartment, I made coffee and headed to my bedroom to take a shower before the day officially got started. My bed was still unmade from leaving the house earlier, but it would have to wait.

In the bathroom, I stripped off my clothes and made the mistake of glancing in the mirror. I looked tired...and sad. And remembering how cute Gina had looked in a big T-shirt after just waking up made me feel more depressed.

I'd been trying to ignore what was really upsetting me about seeing her there, but if I was going to get anything done, I needed to face it.

Gina had spent the night.

And I couldn't forget about seeing the two of them together at the restaurant. Which meant that he and Gina were more than just fuck buddies.

And didn't that make me feel even more pathetic? I had fallen for a guy who I had never really done anything with but have sex. Minus picking up his brother's car, but that had hardly been a date.

I hated feeling this way, and I hated even more that when I saw him later, I was going to have to act normal. If only there was a way to turn off that part of my brain.

I padded slowly to the shower and turned it on. I was giving myself five minutes to cry while I washed myself, and then I needed to get over it and move on because, obviously, Dominick already had.

After getting ready and putting on some armor in the form of a kick-ass pencil skirt and borderline too-sexy-for-work blouse along with stellar makeup and an updo, I headed to work.

After dropping off my briefcase and purse in my office, I stopped to consider who I should ask to take on Dominick's case. I wanted the best for him, but I also wasn't sure how much he'd be able to pay. Some of our attorneys charged more than others. He needed a competent defense counsel, but I didn't want him to go broke.

I decided I would start by considering the people who I would want representing me.

If it were me, I would want me for a lawyer.

I was going to have to rethink my original stance and get used to the fact that I was going to be seeing a lot more of Dominick. It would be hard, but it was the right thing to do.

TWENTY-EIGHT
DOMINICK

It took me several hours, but I made it to Benowitz & St. James by nine a.m. So far, it had been a busy morning.

First, I'd called my job to take a couple of days off work, and then I'd gone to see my mother.

I hadn't wanted to visit my mom at the hospital, but I did it. Vivian had had a point, and even as much as I hated Marjorie, the thought of her suffering alone touched the last thread of empathy I had for her. I didn't go in her room, but I saw enough to know she was being cared for and to speak with the medical staff.

She wasn't doing well and was in a coma. The doctors thought she would survive, but her recovery would be hard. It'd made me all the more determined to get custody of my brother even if it was only until Marjorie was better.

The elevator opened, and a woman smiled at me from behind the desk. "Hi, Dominick."

"Hi, Mara."

"Are you here to pick up some subpoenas?"

"Not today. I'm here to meet Vivian Stern."

Mara's eyebrows rose. "Let me check with her," she said, picking up the phone. "Hi, Ms. Stern. There's a Dominick Reyes to see you." Her eyes widened. "Oh. Okay, I will tell him." She put the phone back on the receiver. "Her assistant is on her way."

"Thank you."

"Mr. Reyes," a woman said before I could even sit.

"That's me."

"Come this way, please."

I followed the woman past large offices and windows to match. We went past a huge conference room with a table that could probably hold twenty people, give or take. I had never been to this part of the firm—I always went down the opposite hallway to Records to pick up subpoenas from Gina—and this was much fancier. This was where the lawyers worked.

We kept going until the offices started getting smaller, and we went to an open area, surrounded by offices with cubicles and desks in the middle.

The woman pointed to an open door. "This is it." She knocked on the wood. "Ms. Stern, Mr. Reyes is here for you."

Vivian's head whipped up from her computer, and she jumped out of her chair. "Thank you, Amanda. Please close the door behind you."

I stepped inside the small office with a single window, and there was a soft click behind me.

The two of us stood almost awkwardly, as if we'd just met. But maybe it was because we'd never seen each other in a professional environment before. Or maybe it was because Vivian had run out of my house this morning like she'd seen a ghost.

"You look—" Vivian cleared her throat. "You look very nice."

I grabbed the sides of my suit jacket and opened it. "Thank you. I thought it'd be best if I dressed up. I know how some people judge me because of my tattoos, and I don't want Spencer to suffer because of that."

Vivian blushed. "Yes, that would be a bad thing."

"So, what do you need me to do?"

"I've been working with someone on the custody issue. I will take you to meet her in a minute. And"—she lifted her chin and smiled—"I've decided that I will be the one to work on your brother's criminal case after all."

"No."

Her expression went blank. "Excuse me?"

"I said, no. I'm going to be the one paying the bills because we both know my mom doesn't have two dimes to rub together, and I want someone else."

Vivian stared at me with her mouth open.

I could understand her confusion. Several hours ago, I had asked her to take my brother's case, and now, I was telling her the opposite. But I'd thought about it. I didn't want her around because she was working for my brother. I wanted her around because of me. Because she wanted to be around me.

"I apologize if this sets us back a little, but I didn't know you were going to change your mind, or I would have texted you."

"No, it's fine. You're the client, which means you're the boss."

I smiled. I liked the sound of that.

"What's funny?" She looked around as if she'd missed something.

"Nothing." I schooled my face. "Do you have anyone in mind who can take Spencer's case?"

"Yes. Now, we'll just have to see if he is free."

I slid my hands into my pockets. "I'm ready when you are."

"Let me collect all my information." Vivian turned around to her desk and put several piles of paper into one bigger one. She straightened. "All right, let's go. We're going to talk to Elaine Rogers first. While you are meeting with her, I will work on finding your brother a lawyer. Sound good?"

"Sounds great."

She took a step forward and stopped. "Oh, do we need to wait for Gina?"

What a strange question. She was my friend, but we weren't that close.

I chuckled at the oddness of it. "No."

Vivian opened her mouth but closed it and tilted her head to the side. With a professional smile, she said, "Let's go then, shall we?" She opened her office door. "It's going to be a long day. I hope you're ready."

"I don't think I have a choice," I said.

Her eyes filled with sympathy. "No, I suppose you don't."

She used one hand to let go of her papers, almost as if she was going to reach out to me, but she pulled back, as if she'd changed her mind.

"Follow me," she said and turned left out of her office door.

TWENTY-NINE
VIVIAN

With a sigh, I set down my briefcase and kicked off my shoes. When I had warned Dominick that today was going to be long, I hadn't made it up, but it had seemed to go on forever.

He had spoken with Elaine, and she had gotten started working on the custody case. I'd found Howard Roguska to take Spencer's case, and he'd wasted no time either. They both had a feeling that by tomorrow night, Spencer would be out of juvie and home with Dominick. I felt very grateful to work with some amazing people.

But I couldn't discount Dominick. He was willing to do everything the lawyers told him to. Without complaint.

"Hot pizza coming through," he said as he pushed open my door.

If only he would listen to me.

I had told him that I didn't need any food, but he had insisted. And while I was starving, I was also tired. I was running on fumes, and I didn't know how much longer I would last before I did something stupid.

Like kiss Dominick even though he was with someone.

I knew it was wrong, but the second I had seen him in a suit, almost all my brain cells had shut off. When my assistant, Amanda, had moved out of the way, all I could remember was standing in front of him like a dolt.

For someone who, at one time, hadn't liked tattoos on men, I almost drooled at the ones that stuck out of Dominick's crisp white shirt. And his black pinstriped suit? I hadn't known whether to curse or thank the gods for delivering such a specimen as Dominick Reyes to my life. But I supposed I really had Gina to thank for that.

Fucking Gina. That was the jealousy talking.

Suddenly cranky and feeling every hour of missed sleep, I took the whole box of pizza into the living room and collapsed onto my couch. Lifting the lid, I reached for a slice and stuck it into my mouth as I slid down and put my feet on the coffee table.

Dominick laughed as he brought over plates, napkins, and two bottles of water. He had taken off his jacket and rolled up the sleeves on his dress shirt, making him even sexier. "I thought you weren't hungry?" he asked.

"I changed my mind," I said with a pout.

He took the box from me and exchanged it for a plate. We ate in silence, and after two pieces, I was still tired, but I was less crabby now that my blood sugar was no longer low.

Since Dominick was still eating, I thought it would be rude to kick him out, so I closed my eyes.

The next thing I knew, I was being lifted off the couch and carried to my bedroom.

"Dominick?" I asked even though it wouldn't be anyone else but him.

"Yeah?"

"You don't have to carry me."

"Too late. We're here."

Gently, he laid me on my bed. Before pulling away, he paused, his face hovering over mine, and I licked my lips. My little nap had given me just enough energy to want sex. It had been so long.

Dominick groaned and stared at me.

"Fuck it," he said and dropped his mouth over mine.

Yes, yes, yes, my pussy screamed from beneath my skirt, where it was getting wet for him.

I went for the buttons on Dominick's shirt but grew impatient, so I pulled at it instead and got hit in the chin by a flying button.

I gasped as he stood back and laughed. His shirt was hanging open from where I'd torn off the buttons.

"Fuck, babe, that was hot." He shrugged off the button-down and kissed me again as he lay down beside me and rolled me to my side. His tongue swept into my mouth, caressing over mine.

How had I lived without tasting him for this long?

Dominick's hand slid up my thigh, under my skirt, and

to my ass. He squeezed one cheek and lifted my leg over his to spread me open. Pulling on the crotch of my panties, he wrapped it around his hand.

I pushed against his chest in a panic, and I blamed my sleepy brain. "Wait. What about your girlfriend?" I hadn't said Gina. I couldn't ask about Gina. Not with the two of us half-naked with each other.

"I don't have a girlfriend," he said and thrust two fingers into me.

"Oh God," I said as I completely forgot my question.

Dominick's thumb rubbed my clit, and I was immediately on the verge of coming.

Over the last two months, I had been spending a lot of time with my vibrator, but it had probably been a week since the last time I'd used it. But even the best toys were nothing compared to flesh and blood.

I buried my face in his chest, and with only a few more strokes, I exploded. My orgasm hit me hard, my muscles tensing everywhere, and I bit Dominick's pec.

He grunted but didn't throw me off.

When my climax waned, he pushed me onto my back and showed me his hand. It glistened from the glow of the streetlights outside. "See that? That's all you." He met my eyes. "For me." He stuck his fingers in his mouth and sucked them off. "It's been way too long."

With a few quick movements, he got rid of my skirt and underwear. When he pushed my legs wide, the cool air hit me, letting me know just how wet I was.

Dominick fell to his stomach and put his mouth right on my pussy without any additional foreplay, as if he just had to taste me again.

I was sensitive but also ready, as if my clit would burst if I didn't come again.

Dominick lifted his head for a moment. "Unbutton your shirt and take off your bra. I want you to play with your nipples while I eat your cunt."

Not one to let a good idea get away, I did as he'd directed. My breasts were full and felt heavy in my hands. My nipples were tight, and I moaned as I twisted them with my fingertips.

Dominick's tongue flicked over my swollen bud, lifting me higher and higher. And when he sucked it into his mouth, I shattered again. My back arched, and I threw my head back as I ground my pussy against his mouth.

I'd never had two great orgasms in a row before, and I'd never felt farther away yet more connected to my body.

Dominick crawled up me, and I heard the sound of a buckle clinking and a zipper being undone. He brushed one finger down my cheek. "Vivian?"

I blinked up at him. "Hmm?"

"You said you're on birth control, right?"

I nodded.

"And you haven't been with anyone else since me?"

It was a question, but I answered it with one of my own. "How did you know?"

"You haven't come that hard since our first time together." He wrapped his arms around me. "Besides, I just *know*." His last word was emphasized as he drove his cock into me.

He didn't wait for me to adjust—not that he needed to because I was so wet. He just lifted my legs over his hips and began to ride me.

"Harder," I found myself saying. It was like I couldn't get enough of him. I wanted to feel it to the point of pain.

Dominick must have been holding a part of himself back because he pounded into me with such force that I felt him hit my cervix. I held on to him, wanting him to feel as good as he made me feel, but he surprised me again by making me come for a third time.

Dragging my nails down his back, I gripped him tightly, as if I was worried he was going to leave me. But he rode me through my climax, my nether muscles hurting from contracting so hard.

Dominick grunted and plunged into me one last time. His dick swelled inside me, and I could feel it jerk with each jet of his release. Just before he was done, he quickly pulled out and commanded me to, "Open."

My jaw dropped, and he pushed the head of his cock into my mouth as the last stream of cum was released.

The two of us together was something I'd never experienced before, and I sucked on him, trying to get every last drop.

With a groan, he dragged his shaft away and dropped down beside me.

As he pulled me into his arms, I said, "You didn't use a condom, did you?"

"Nope." He didn't even try to deny it.

I meant to ask more, but my body was done, and I quickly fell asleep.

THIRTY

VIVIAN

I'd woken up alone, and if the other side of the bed hadn't been messed up, I would have thought I'd imagined last night. I'd known Dominick had to get up early because he had to meet with Elaine, and it was kind of a relief to be by myself.

The sex...the sex had been...I didn't even have the words. *The best I've ever had,* came to mind, but that sounded cheesy.

It didn't really matter because it couldn't happen again. I knew Dominick had said he didn't have a girlfriend, but obviously, something was going on with him and Gina. And the guilt was really messing with me.

Also, we hadn't used a condom last night...again. Not only had I had to change my sheets before work, but I also had to talk to Dominick about STIs. And Gina. She deserved to know her partner was having unprotected sex.

I sighed as I sat back in my chair.

Currently, I was hiding out in my office, not wanting to face anyone, but I didn't have a choice.

There was a knock at my door.

"Come in," I said.

Amanda popped her head in. "Dominick Reyes is here to see you again."

"Let him in. Thanks."

Amanda stepped aside, let Dominick enter, and shut the door behind her as she left.

"Hey," he said and smiled at me. It was casual, but I saw a little smirk too. One that said, *I remember every dirty thing I did to you last night, and I know you remember it too.*

I had to look away before my body took over my brain, and that was when I noticed he was wearing another suit. This one was blue and looked just as good on him.

What is a welder doing with so many suits? It's not fair.

I pinched the bridge of my nose and closed my eyes. I needed to create some boundaries with this man. I couldn't go on like this. I couldn't share him with anyone, but I couldn't take him away from anyone either.

"You okay, babe?" Dominick asked.

"No." I dropped my hand on my desk and looked up. "Dominick—"

There was another knock at my door, and this time, it opened without anyone waiting for me to say something.

"Is Dominick in here?" Elaine asked, looking around. "Oh." She laughed when she saw him and stepped farther inside. "Are you ready to go?"

He nodded. "Yeah. I was just making sure that Vivian was going to be there." His look of expectation reminded me of a little boy who was afraid he was going to be disappointed again.

I didn't know why he wanted me to be there so badly, but I didn't have it in me to tell him no. Besides, there wouldn't be any sex in a courtroom full of people. I'd be safe from getting naked with him for a while.

"Yes, I'll be there. I'll head over soon."

Dominick followed Elaine out, and I knew I had to leave soon too.

I went to the break room to get a Diet Pepsi out of the vending machine. I'd had coffee already that morning, but I needed more caffeine.

I was almost to the break room when I recognized Gina's voice. I quickly stopped, turned around, and headed back the way I had come. I could find something to drink somewhere else. That was, until I heard Gina say something that made me stop in my tracks.

"We're moving in together," she said.

"No way. You two haven't been dating that long. I remember when you were telling me about your first date."

"I know. But we spend so much time together, and I love him. He's the best boyfriend, and if we're going to get married someday, I need to live with him first."

I could hear the smile in Gina's voice, and I felt sick for two reasons. My heart was breaking again, and Gina's was going to be too. I was also pissed that Dominick had lectured me about lying to him when I hadn't, and he was doing the same to me and Gina.

My phone buzzed in my hand.

D Appointment: Are you on your way?

I gave my phone the finger because I didn't want to say anything before the hearing started. What was that old saying? *You don't shit where you eat.* And I was not going to be blamed for him not getting custody.

Me: Soon. I'll be there ASAP.

The stupid white lie somehow made me feel better, but only for a minute. I hated that I was getting satisfaction out of being petty.

I let out a breath of frustration.

This wasn't me. Being jealous, heartbroken, and petty. I wasn't that kind of person when it came to men. This needed to end.

I spun around and marched into the break room.

"Gina," I said, interrupting her conversation with someone.

The two of them were standing against the kitchen counter. The other woman turned, and I saw it was Mara.

Of course it was Mara. She and Gina had been there at the beginning. It seemed fitting they would be here at the end.

"What's up, Stern?" Gina said, putting her hand on her hip.

"Gina, I really hate to be the one to tell you this, but your boyfriend is cheating on you."

Mara gasped.

Gina dropped her hand and stood straight. "Excuse me?" she said.

I didn't know if her tone was one of *how dare you accuse my man of such a thing* or *what do you know, and when are you going to tell me everything.*

"I know we're not friends, and you're going to hate me now, but I can't let you move in with...him." I couldn't say Dominick's name. Keeping it to pronouns made it less difficult to say.

"And how do you know this?" Gina asked.

Okay, she didn't believe me, so I was just going to have to say it.

"Because we slept together last night. Not like sleeping. You know, the other kind. Sex. I mean, we did sleep together, too, but that's not the point. The point is, he was with me all night, and we had sex." I raised my eyebrows. "A lot. And it was unprotected." I shook my head sadly. "I'm sorry, but he's not faithful to you."

Mara looked back and forth between the two of us. "Wow. I did not take you for the other woman," she said to me.

"I didn't know I was, okay? I hadn't seen him in two months." I lifted my hand toward her friend. "I mean, Gina was the one who set me up with him. How was I supposed to know they'd fall in love?" I dropped my arm and looked at Gina. "It is really weird that you would set me up with a guy you like. Also, if you love him so much, why aren't you at his hearing? Why aren't you supporting him?"

That last part bothered me. Cheater or not, Dominick was the only dependable person Spencer had in his life, and Dominick was a good brother.

Gina put her hand on her stomach, threw her head back, and laughed.

"Oh my God," Mara said to me. "You broke her."

"Gina, I'm sorry. I shouldn't have put any blame on you. This is all Dominick's fault. He's a grown-ass man who knows better. I mean, he didn't even try to hide it."

What kind of guy had his girlfriend come out of the bedroom in front of the other woman? And what did that say about the other woman who believed him when he said he didn't have a girlfriend?

I was just as much to blame.

Mara's panicked look turned to one of confusion. She wrinkled her nose. "Dominick? Gina's not dating Dominick. She's dating Tony."

THIRTY-ONE
VIVIAN

Hold up.

"Who's Tony?" I asked, completely dumbfounded.

"Gina's boyfriend," Mara said as if I was a complete moron.

Gina finally calmed down enough to be able to speak even though she was still laughing. "Tony is Dominick's friend."

"But...I saw you and Dominick together at a restaurant two months ago. And he had turned me down because he had plans." *Did I imagine the whole thing?*

Gina's eyes slowly widened. "Oh shit. Was this a while back when you got all snotty with me?"

I lifted a shoulder. "Well, I wouldn't say snotty. I might have been...a little short-tempered," I admitted.

"You were not fun to be around," Mara said.

"Thank you, Mara. That was very helpful," I said in a flat tone.

She lifted her hands up. "I was just sayin'.'"

"I don't know what you saw, but *Tony* and I went out to eat with Dominick before we all went to a concert together. At the restaurant, Tony had stopped to look at something on his tire because he's obsessed with his car." Gina rolled her eyes. "But he was right behind us. You would have seen him if you had stuck around for a few seconds longer."

A memory resurfaced of me literally running into a man on my way out of the restaurant and thinking he looked familiar, but being too focused on getting home, I'd forgotten about it.

"Oh crap." I pulled out a chair at the nearest table, fell into it, and put my head in my hands.

There was a possibility I had entirely fucked up.

I was a lawyer. Innocent until proven guilty was kind of our motto, and here, I had jumped to conclusions about Dominick and Gina without seeing all the evidence.

"I'm still shocked Dominick had unprotected sex with you. That man has condoms stashed everywhere. You must be important or something."

I barely heard Gina's remark because I was thinking about yesterday morning.

Still confused, I leaned back in my chair. "But what about yesterday morning? You had obviously slept over."

"*Tony* and I slept over. We'd come over the night before and had a little too much to drink, so we crashed in Dominick's guest room." Gina laughed. "Tony does exist, I swear."

"I know. I kind of met him."

"You met him?" Gina howled with laughter. "Wait until I tell Dominick this. If he loses the custody hearing, at least he'll have this to brighten his day."

I flew up from my seat so fast that the chair skidded backward. "Shit. The hearing. I have to go." I ran for the door but paused before turning the corner. "And please don't tell him about this. I'm embarrassed enough as it is."

Gina nodded and waved, so I hurried away.

I couldn't be sure, but I thought I heard Mara ask, "You're totally going to tell him, aren't you?"

But I was too far away to hear Gina's answer.

DOMINICK

The judge took her seat behind the bench, and Vivian was not in the courtroom yet.

I was trying not to be nervous, but if this hearing didn't go well, I wouldn't be able to see Spencer in juvie. And right now, he was there all alone. The only person who had visited him was his new lawyer.

A squeak sounded behind me, and I looked over my shoulder to see Vivian sneak in and practically tiptoe to an open seat several rows back. She sat down and gave me two thumbs-up, and I felt a little less nervous.

Elaine stood and gestured for me to follow. "Good morning, Judge St. James. We are here to petition that the custody of Spencer Reyes be granted to Dominick Reyes. His mother is currently in the hospital in a coma, and his father isn't in the picture..."

I admired the speech my lawyer had put together, but I found myself tuning out, unable to pay attention. I couldn't help but wonder what would happen to my brother if the judge said no.

"Mr. Reyes?" the judge said, and I almost missed it until Elaine looked at me.

"Yes, Your Honor?"

"You have a steady job that will pay for the needs of a teenager?"

"Yes, ma'am. I work full-time as a welder at Unify Manufacturing and part-time as a process server to various firms in Minneapolis."

Every place I worked was listed for the judge to see, but I hoped she wouldn't have to go through them all individually.

"And you understand that if I grant you this, it is only temporary? Either Spencer's mother will resume custody or you will have to refile."

"Yes."

The judge picked up a piece of paper. "Your employer has sent a letter attesting to your professionalism and trustworthiness."

My attorney had said she was going to request this, but I hadn't realized she'd gotten it in time. I would have to thank my supervisor the next time I saw him. And maybe get him a gift card or something.

"While I do appreciate the letter of recommendation, Mr. Reyes, I would like to hear from more than one person. Your criminal record, while old, does concern me when I have to consider placing a child in your custody. Is there someone from your personal life that can vouch for you?"

I looked at my attorney for help. We hadn't talked about having a backup, but I supposed we should have.

"I'll ask for a continuance since this isn't something normally required," she whispered to me. She looked to the judge, and in a normal voice, she said, "I'm sorry, Your Honor—"

"I'm here, Your Honor."

Elaine and I turned around to see Vivian standing up.

"Ms. Stern, it's nice to see you in my courtroom," Judge St. James said.

How does the judge know Vivian?

"Please approach the bench and have a seat in the witness stand."

Vivian smiled at me as she passed me and sat down.

"Please state your name and occupation."

"Vivian Stern. I'm an attorney at...Benowitz & St. James."

I noticed the hesitation in Vivian's voice, and I wondered if it had to do with the *St. James* in her firm's name and the name of the judge. But Judge St. James seemed unfazed by Vivian's employer.

"Do you know Mr. Reyes in a professional or personal sense?"

"Personal."

"Even though he has been a process server for your firm?"

"Correct. I met him outside the office and have never personally worked with him."

"And how long have you known Mr. Reyes?" the judge asked.

"Unfortunately, not long. Less than six months."

"And how do you know he would be an appropriate guardian to his brother?"

"Dominick—Mr. Reyes—was the one who took Spencer to the hospital when he broke his arm, and he took care of him afterward. He obviously cares about his brother. Mr. Reyes is single and childless, and he is willing to pay someone to help him get custody. Big brothers don't do that unless they love their siblings."

Last night, I had expressed with my body how much I wanted this woman, but hearing the words she said up there sealed the deal.

She was mine.

Now, I just needed to make sure she knew that.

My dick throbbed at all the ways I was going to show her that she belonged to me.

I unobtrusively adjusted myself in my suit pants.

Judge St. James looked to the family services side of the court. "Do you have any questions for this witness?"

"Not at this time."

"Ms. Stern, you may step down."

Vivian left the witness stand, gave me another smile, and went back to her seat behind me.

"Mr. Reyes," Judge St. James said, folding her hands and placing them on her bench.

She looked serious, and I had a feeling it didn't bode well for me.

"I always want to do what is in the best interest of a child, and in this case, I think having you as his guardian is just that." She picked up her gavel and hit it.

Relief swept through my body, making me almost light-headed.

Elaine put her hand on my arm. "I'll file the paperwork immediately, so you can visit Spencer as soon as possible."

"Thank you. Thank you so much for everything."

"I'm glad it all worked out."

I spun around to see Vivian wasn't in the courtroom anymore. I was worried that she'd left, but I found her out in the hallway, staring down at her phone.

"Hey," I said.

She looked up at me, concern in her eyes. "Oh. Hey." She smiled when she saw it was me. "Congratulations."

I really wanted to kiss her, but there were too many people around. "Thank you. I don't know if I could have done it without you."

She blushed. "I think you would have been fine. Judge St. James is a good person."

"Have you worked with her before?"

"Yes, but not in a courtroom. It's kind of a long story." She bit her lip, as if something was bothering her.

"Are you okay?"

She huffed. "Me? I should be asking you that."

"I'm better now." I looked at my watch. "But listen, I need to go. I'll see you later, okay?"

"Sure, sure."

I picked up one of her hands, lacing our fingers together. "No, baby, when I say I'm going to see you later, I mean it."

THIRTY-TWO

VIVIAN

Speechless, I stood there as Dominick kissed the back of my hand and left.

He'd called me baby. Not the shortened babe. But *baby*.

What is going on?

My phone buzzed in my hand.

> Delaney: I can do an early lunch. Meet me in 20 at the Italian place.

I put my hand on my chest in relief.

After the hearing, I had messaged her right away, asking her if she would meet me. I wanted to explain to her in person about why I hadn't told her I worked with her ex-husband.

Telling her in front of a courtroom full of people was not a way I had ever pictured it happening, and I was angry with myself for not saying something earlier.

I'd thought for sure she would tell me to give her some time or maybe even not reply until she was no longer upset with me.

Finding out she was willing to hear me out right away made me feel better. But only a little. I still had to apologize.

The restaurant was only about ten minutes away, so I got a table, ordered two waters, and waited for Delaney to show up. I didn't do patient well, and by the time she got there, I had ripped apart two napkins.

"You got something on your mind?" she asked, seeing the mess I had made on the table. "Do you need to talk about it?" she asked, taking the chair next to me.

Delaney was mature and sophisticated. She wasn't that much older than me, but sometimes, I felt like she was a mom and I was a kid.

I turned in my seat toward her, so she could see my face. "I asked you here, so I could apologize to you in person. I'm a horrible friend and person to work with. I should have never kept it a secret, and I'm sorry for not telling you."

Delaney took a sip of her water, and I copied her out of nervousness. "Sorry for what? Sorry for not telling me you've clearly been boning that beautiful man who was in my courtroom today?"

I clapped my hand over my mouth, almost spitting out the water I had just drunk. Maybe I was wrong about Delaney being sophisticated.

"Uh...no, I wasn't talking about Dominick. I was referring to the fact that I never told you where I worked. That I work with your ex-husband." I looked down at my hands. "And I apologize."

She laughed, and wasn't that just great? Everyone was laughing at me today.

"Vivian, I know you work with my ex-husband."

My head flew up. "You do?"

"Yes. My ex and I are both friends with the mayor and her husband. There was a reason she asked me to be a part of her pilot program. And she went to Preston and asked him to recommend someone from his firm because she knew him." She tilted her head. "You really thought I didn't know?"

It seemed silly now to think that she'd really had no idea where I worked after we'd been working together for so long.

"Do I have to say yes?"

She laughed again.

"I can't believe I didn't figure it out."

"You should have because I know everything," she said with a grin.

"What did I miss?"

I looked up to see Rayne pulling out a chair. Since I hadn't told her to come, Delaney must have invited her.

"I was just waiting for Vivian over here to tell me if her boyfriend had as many tattoos under his suit as he did sticking out of it," Delaney said with a smirk.

Rayne's jaw dropped. "You have a boyfriend? With tattoos?"

Delaney waved a finger at her neck. "They were visible around his collar and his sleeves." She pointed to her wrist. "Yum."

"Vivian." Rayne smacked my arm. "You've been holding out on us."

"No, I haven't. We're not like that."

Rayne frowned. "We aren't? I mean, I've been telling the two of you about my boyfriend since the day we met."

I shook my head. "No. I mean, Dominick and me. We're not boyfriend and girlfriend."

Delaney snorted. "Bullshit."

"We're not."

She looked at Rayne. "If you saw the way this man looked at Vivian, you would know exactly what I mean."

I thought Delaney was exaggerating, but I also wanted her to tell me exactly what she meant down to the very last detail.

She leaned toward the middle of the table. "Let's just say, if the two of them had been alone, I have no doubt Vivian would have been on her back, naked, with that man inside her."

"Oh my God, Delaney," I said while Rayne covered her mouth and laughed.

"I feel like I really missed out today," she said.

Delaney threw a hand out. "What? You think just because I'm a judge and a mom, I don't have sex? Preston and I used to have so much sex." She stared off into the distance. "It's probably the reason we didn't divorce sooner." She looked back at us. "But I do admit, it's been too long. I miss it."

"Please, tell us about him," Rayne said. "I need some good news on the romance front."

"I thought you and your boyfriend were going on a trip together?" I asked.

"I don't want to talk about it right now. I want to hear about this sexy guy."

"There's not much to tell. My coworker introduced me to him because I was looking for a little bedroom action. We were getting together whenever we felt the urge until I called it off about two months ago."

Delaney raised her eyebrows. "Wait. You just vouched for a guy you called things off with? Do I need to rethink my decision?"

I could tell she was joking, but I still said, "*No*," a little too forcefully. "I mean, whatever is or isn't going on with us, it has nothing to do with his brother."

"Ahh," Rayne said.

"What?" I dared to ask.

"You care about him."

I shrugged and rolled my eyes. "I suppose I do."

"So, why did you call it off?" Delaney asked.

"We are so different. And he was never supposed to be anything other than a—"

My phone buzzed on the table.

"D Appointment," Rayne finished.

"How did you know?" I asked.

She grinned and pointed to my phone. "Because he

just texted you." She laughed. "You have his name as *D Appointment* in your phone?"

"I told you, we were just having sex. And he put his name in like that on my phone, not me."

"But you didn't change it?" Rayne pointed out.

"What did the text say?" Delaney asked.

"Something about him getting a text and needing to talk to Vivian later." Rayne's eyes widened, and she fanned her face. "I don't think I should say the rest out loud in public."

She had to be teasing me.

"I don't believe you." Swiping my phone off the table, I opened my text messages.

> D Appointment: I just got the craziest text. You and I need to talk later. My fucking cock is aching to be inside that sweet cunt of yours again.

"Let me see," Delaney said, taking my phone out of my hand. She whistled. "He has got it bad."

I snatched my phone back. "No, he doesn't."

"Why are you fighting this?" Delaney asked.

"I don't know. We're just so different. We come from separate worlds."

Although learning that Dominick was a process server and did work for my firm had been very surprising, I wondered if the day I'd thought I saw him wasn't just a figment of my imagination. But that was beside the point. We were still unalike in many ways.

"I don't know how we'd ever work as a couple." I sighed after saying the thing that had been bothering me all along. "At some point, he might realize he's more fun and a lot cooler than me and get rid of my basic-bitch ass." I scoffed. "Or I'm going to get sick of him not picking up after himself or doing the dishes. I've seen his house." I shrugged. "And I'd rather not be around when that happens."

THIRTY-THREE
DOMINICK

Tapping my foot, I waited impatiently for my brother. I hated that he was all alone and that I hadn't been able to see him sooner.

When he came through the door, the look on his face when he saw me was worth the last two days of hard work.

I pulled him into a hug. "I came as soon as I could."

Spencer stepped back, so we could sit. "I know. I was told that only parents and guardians were allowed to be here. I didn't even expect to see you."

I held out my hands. "Surprise. I'm your temporary guardian."

"And all it took was for Mom to end up in the hospital."

I raised my eyebrows.

He looked away. "I'm sorry."

"It is what it is."

"I didn't do it, you know."

"Spencer, I never thought you did."

"I did spray-paint Mom's car though."

I was shocked because he had always been so passive when it came to our mother. He'd never fought her on anything.

"What made you so mad that you wrote *Bitch* on her car? I feel like that is something I would have done when I was your age. Not you."

He lowered his head. "I was just so mad."

"What about?"

"She didn't pay the electric bill again. All our food went bad, and my friend said I could spend the weekend with him, but Mom said no. It feels like she wants me to suffer sometimes."

I folded my hands and rested my forehead on them for a moment to contain my rage at the selfish woman who had given birth to us. When I felt calm enough, I looked back up. "Why didn't you tell me?"

"Because I'm not your responsibility, Dom. You do enough for me as it is. You're supposed to be living your own life. Not taking care of some sixteen-year-old."

"But you're not some sixteen-year-old. You're my brother, and I love you. Yes, Marjorie should be doing a better job, but she's not, and I want to help you. No one is forcing me."

"I know, but I still feel bad."

"Please don't. Marjorie should feel bad, but you shouldn't."

I knew that was easier said than done.

"Is Mom okay?"

"She's unconscious right now. She hasn't woken up."

Spencer's lips quivered. "Is she going to be okay?"

I hated that he was sad for someone who didn't deserve it.

"She might be. She will have some permanent scars, but most of the damage was smoke."

And her lungs had already been shit, so I wasn't sure how much it really mattered.

"Have you visited her?"

"Once." I didn't tell him I hadn't gone inside the hospital room.

"Will you go again?"

I didn't want to visit her any more than I had to.

"For me?" he asked.

I couldn't say no to my brother. "Yes. But in the meantime, I want you to know I have someone working on your case. Tomorrow, the fire inspector is supposed to go investigate the trailer. I'm hoping this will clear your name."

"What about the vandalism?"

I shrugged. "I'm not sure. They might drop all the charges. Your lawyer says we need to worry about the big charges first. Vandalism is a misdemeanor, not a felony."

He nodded. "That makes sense."

"In all this, where's Marjorie's boyfriend? Why aren't they looking at him?"

"He took off a couple of weeks ago. You know how it goes. I'm pretty sure he's in Reno or something now, so he probably has a solid alibi."

"Fuck," I muttered under my breath. "Look, Spencer, I don't want you giving up. We're going to work on getting you out of here on bail soon."

He sat back and crossed his arms over his chest, his mouth set in a tight line. "No."

I frowned. "What do you mean, no? Why wouldn't you want to get out of here?"

"You're not spending any more money on me, Dominick. There is no way my bail is going to be cheap."

I gritted my teeth. "Don't worry about that."

He stood. "I said, no. If you do this, I will never speak to you again."

I almost didn't go to the hospital because I was so mad at my brother.

I understood his concern. I just didn't agree with it. I didn't want him to spend any more time in juvie than he had to, and if that meant putting a lien on my house or something, I was willing to do it.

Then again, I was so pissed at him that I almost didn't care if he stayed right where he was.

Kids, man.

The elevator doors opened, and I turned right to find Marjorie's room. My plan was to tell her Spencer loved her and was thinking about her and to get the hell out of there. Then get to Vivian's before she went to bed.

But you know what they say about plans.

When I arrived at Marjorie's room, there were half a dozen medical staff in there.

"What's going on?"

All of them turned at the sound of my voice.

A man in a white coat—a doctor, I'd guess—stepped forward. "And you are?"

"Dominick. Dominick Reyes. I'm Marjorie Reyes's son."

The doctor exchanged looks with the other staff. "Dominick, does your mother drink by chance?"

I could tell the man was trying to be tactful in his approach, but there was no need.

I scoffed. "Like a fish. Among other things. Prescription drugs and probably some illegal ones too." I crossed my arms over my chest. "Why?"

"Your mother had a seizure this morning, something that seems unrelated to her injuries. We ran some tests, and her blood work is all over the place. But now that we know there's a possible reason for the seizure, we know where to go from here," he said with a reassuring smile.

But a seizure didn't sound so reassuring to me. It sounded scary. A lot scarier than some burns. I didn't want to care, but I was worried.

I dropped my hands to my sides. "What does this mean?"

"It means your mother is going through withdrawal. The good news is, she's in a hospital, where we can properly manage it and supervise her. We will have to keep her in a coma though. She still hasn't regained consciousness, and we'll make sure she stays that way until she's no longer withdrawing."

"So, Marjorie is going to wake up from this...sober?"

"That's right. But it won't happen overnight."

I nodded my head.

"And with her burns, it might make her recovery longer, but we suspect she will get better. From both." He looked around again. "We were just getting ready to leave, if you want to come in to sit with her."

I found myself nodding my head again. I didn't want to sit with her. But I also didn't *not* want to sit with her.

As the medical staff cleared out of the room, I pulled up a chair and felt something I hadn't felt in a long time when it came to the woman who had given birth to me.

Hope.

THIRTY-FOUR
VIVIAN

D Appointment: Hey.

I STARED DOWN AT MY PHONE AND TYPED BACK.

Me: Hey.

D Appointment: I'm going to be later
tonight than I thought. I'm with my mom.

My breath caught. I couldn't believe Dominick was
with his mother. And he'd referred to her as his "mom." I
had so many questions. But I sensed now was not the time
to pry.

I also didn't really know what he'd meant by "later
tonight." I knew he wanted to talk to me when he had a
chance, but we didn't have plans. But again, I wouldn't ask.
His mom was in the hospital, and he only needed support
right now.

Me: I completely understand. I hope your mother is doing well.

D Appointment: Thanks, baby. Later.

I closed my eyes. There was that *baby* again. I got a little tingle up my spine, seeing him write that.

I turned my screen off and set my phone down. "Again, Vivian, not the time," I lectured myself.

Someone walking by my office stopped and came back. "Were you talking to me?"

I waved them off. "No."

They shrugged and kept going.

Turning back to my computer, I tried to think of work. Or rather, I tried to think of anything other than Dominick.

Thankfully, I was able to concentrate on work and finally left the building at around seven. I went home, had a salad for dinner, and cleaned my apartment. But it didn't stop me from wondering how things were going with Dominick.

Dominick

The gravel under my car tires crunched as I approached my mom's trailer. I had yet to inspect it, and something had called me there tonight.

The sun had set, so I aimed my headlights on the home and got as close as the crime scene tape would allow.

As I got out of my vehicle, I saw my mother's beat-up car with the big word *Bitch* sprayed across it. And about fifty feet away was the burned shell of where my brother and our mom used to live. I hadn't realized it was completely destroyed. I didn't think there could even be anything salvageable left inside.

I took a seat on the hood of my car and stared. It had been a long day. Seeing my little brother locked up and then seeing my mother up close in her hospital bed. Everything had become more real to me. Not that it hadn't been before, but now, it seemed like there was no denying, no putting in the back of my mind what was happening to my family.

I ran my hand over my face and hung my head. The stress of it all felt heavy, but I was the only person they had.

Sometimes, I wondered what it would have been like if my parents hadn't gotten into an accident. Would they still be married? Would my mother have never started drinking? Would I have a father to help me in situations like these?

But then Spencer probably would have never been born, and I didn't regret my brother coming into my life.

And now, with my mother detoxing in the hospital, there was a chance she might stay sober. I knew it was a long shot, but one of the hardest steps was making it through the withdrawal period. Maybe once she did that, she would see how much Spencer needed her.

I sighed. *Fuck.* Everything was such a mess. And life definitely wasn't fair.

The burned trailer proved that.

Because the very thing that could ruin my brother's life could be the very thing that saved my mother's.

I sat for way too long at my mother's, ruminating in my thoughts. When I finally left, I realized how late it had gotten. I was sure that Vivian had gone to bed by now since tomorrow was a workday. I had to go back to my job myself. I didn't know what else was going to come up, and I needed to save as many vacation hours as I could. It seemed our talk would have to wait for another day.

When I got to Vivian's, I used the spare key I'd swiped that morning from her key hook in the kitchen to unlock the door and let myself in. This morning, I had wanted to make sure the door and the dead bolt were secured before I left since she was still sleeping. I had intended to give it back to her, but forgetting had come in handy.

I brushed my teeth with the toothbrush I had picked up on the way to her apartment and padded lightly to her room. There was enough light for me to see her sprawled out across the middle of the bed, and I smiled. For some reason, I pictured her sleeping neatly on one side of the mattress.

After stripping off my clothes, I climbed into bed with Vivian, only to frown at what I found there.

"Dom?" she asked in a sleepy voice as I tugged at her pajamas.

"Yeah?"

"What are you doing?"

Her bottoms went flying toward the wall with her top right behind it.

"Getting you naked, babe. When you sleep with me, there won't be anything between us," I explained, pulling her into my arms.

"That's not what I—never mind," she said and nestled her head on my chest.

"Just one more thing, and then you can go back to sleep."

"Hmm?" she murmured.

I picked up her leg and drew it over my hip as I slowly pushed my stiff cock inside her beautiful cunt.

Perfect.

I ran my hand over the back of her head. "Just what I needed."

And with that, I fell right asleep.

THIRTY-FIVE
VIVIAN

BEFORE I KNEW IT, A WEEK HAD PASSED. THINGS WERE going well at work. I finally brought up the subject of me working with Delaney in the Women in Law program in front of Preston. Now that I had talked to her about it, I felt the need to speak with him as well.

He simply shrugged and said, "I kind of figured since she and the mayor are friends." He looked over at me, eyebrows pulled together. "It's not a problem, is it?"

I waved my hands back and forth in haste. "No. Not at all."

"Good," he said with a nod and pulled out a container of food and popped it into the microwave.

And that was the end of that. I had worried for nothing.

So, everything seemed normal from the outside. My job was going great, the Women in Law project was going well, and my sister had told me she was coming home to visit sometime soon, but for her, that could mean next week to six months from now. The only thing that didn't make sense was Dominick spending every night in my apartment. I would almost say he'd moved in, except I didn't see him much during the day.

He got up much earlier than me for work, and he was picking up overtime while I often worked late. Sometimes, I came home to him sleeping in my bed.

The whole situation confused me, especially since we never had the "talk" he had texted me about. But maybe I had misunderstood the message he'd sent. And my every intention of talking to him had flown out the window as soon as I found out he and Gina weren't involved. But it didn't change that we had no defined relationship status, yet we were having unprotected sex almost every night.

But I knew why I hadn't spoken up. I didn't want him to go.

I'd done the unthinkable and developed feelings for Dominick Reyes.

Hard-core, *I'd give up everything, I love you* feelings for a man who I'd never thought I'd fall for in a million years.

But all good things came to an end, and waiting for this fling we were having to come to a conclusion was starting to wear on me.

Tonight, I got off work at a decent time, and Dominick had said he'd meet me at my apartment for dinner. I thought I would beat him home, but I was surprised to find him standing in the living room when I got there.

His back was to me, so I set my purse and briefcase down and said his name. "Dominick."

He spun around and put a finger up. He was on the phone.

"Yeah. Yeah." He nodded and grinned. "Thank you. Yes. Tomorrow." He pulled the phone away, hit End, and shouted, "*Fuck yeah.*"

"What happened?" I asked.

He slowly walked toward me, and with every step, he said a word. "The fire investigation is complete. No accelerants were found. The most likely cause was a cigarette."

My hands flew up to my mouth. "Oh my God, Dominick, that is excellent news."

"I know," he said, reaching me and grabbing my hips. "I mean, I believed my brother when he said he didn't do it. I just didn't think it would be this easy to prove."

I threw my arms around his neck and hugged him. "I am so happy for your brother." I stepped back on my heels. "And you too, of course. This is amazing."

"I know."

"So, what happens now?"

"Howard said he is pushing the district attorney's office to release Spencer right away. He could be out as soon as tomorrow. I don't know what they'll do about the vandalism charge, but that isn't enough to hold him." He met my eyes. "Right?"

"I would think not." I sniffled. "That is such a relief."

"Holy shit, Vivian, are you crying?"

"Of course not," I said with a laugh, wiping a tear from my eye before it fell to my cheek.

Dominick laughed too. "I didn't think you had it in you."

"What?"

"Crying."

"Ha-ha." If he only knew. I'd bawled after I saw Gina at his house the morning I went to tell him about Spencer. And, now, I felt like crying again, knowing he was going to go back home to take care of his brother.

I was going to miss him.

He squeezed my hips and looked around. "What's for dinner? Should we go out and celebrate?"

I didn't know how long I was going to be able to keep on a happy face. Dominick was going to leave now that his brother was getting out of the juvenile detention center and would need a place to stay.

Their mother was improving, but it would probably be a couple more weeks before she got out of the hospital, and we had no idea if she'd get custody back right away or not.

It seemed this was the end of Dominick and me.

Suddenly, I was angry with myself for caring so much. I'd never felt this way with my ex, who I'd spent years with, and I shouldn't feel this way now.

I rubbed my head. "Can you give me a few minutes? I just have a headache."

His brow furrowed. "Are you okay?"

I smiled reassuringly. "Yes. It's just a headache. Not fun, but not the end of the world."

"Yeah, it's fine if we wait. No rush. Do you want me to get you anything?"

"No. I have pain pills in the bedroom. I'll get them when I go and change." I headed toward my room. "I'll be back."

I turned toward the hallway, then glanced back to make sure Dominick didn't follow me. He went toward my spare bedroom and looked around instead. I was a little confused about what he was doing, but I didn't want to waste my moment to escape.

I stripped off my work clothes and uncomfortable bra and went to find something nice yet comfortable to put on for dinner, but I ended up sitting on my bed instead. I should have told Dominick I didn't feel like eating.

"Hey, Viv?"

I jumped up, grabbed my silk robe, threw it over my underwear, and ran to the bathroom. But I wasn't fast enough.

"What were you doing, just sitting there?"

THIRTY-SIX
VIVIAN

I swung around and grabbed the lapels of my robe. It was short, only going to the tops of my thighs, so I tried to compensate by pulling it tighter.

"Uh...I was going to brush my teeth."

"What did I say about lying to me?" Dominick tilted his head. "You know, I still haven't properly punished you for lying to me two months ago when you ditched me."

My mouth fell open, and I stepped backward while he advanced on me until my butt hit the bathroom counter.

Putting my hand up to try to stop him, I said, "Okay, but why would I lie about brushing my teeth? I've been at work all day. Maybe I want fresh breath before dinner. Also, I think you punished me when you came to my door and *fucked* me without a *condom*. And I'm not your child. You can be mad at me if I lied to you, but you can't punish me."

Dominick pulled my hand off his chest, where it had

landed, and picked me up to sit on the counter. "I don't know why you would lie about brushing your teeth either." He pushed my legs apart and scooted in between them. "I just know you did." He lowered his voice. "I can tell when you're lying." He raised his voice to a normal level again. "As for two months ago"—he grabbed my robe and pulled it apart—"fucking you wasn't punishment."

He pinched my nipple, and I yelped.

"You'd know if I was punishing you. Making you come on my cock is not it."

He squeezed my other nipple, but this time, I was ready, so I stayed quiet.

"As for the no condom, that was an accident."

Without warning, he grabbed the sides of my panties and ripped them off.

I gasped. More in surprise that they had given out so easily than in him actually doing it.

He looked down, as if he was analyzing his handiwork. "I think your punishment should be no underwear for a week," he said, as if thinking out loud. "That way, I can fuck you whenever I want."

"*Dominick.*"

His head whipped up. "Make it a month."

I stuck out my chin. "That's impossible. What about my period?"

He seemed to give it real consideration, as if he had control over what I wore. "You can wear it while you're bleeding, but you're still fucking me every night."

"You cannot be serious."

He scoffed and made a face of disgust. "Is this another thing your ex wouldn't do?"

"Him and a lot of other people."

"Hmm. I don't care about blood and that crap." He tossed my underwear, or what was left of it, in the small garbage can in the corner. "We're fucking."

I was beginning to wonder if he'd lost his mind. Gone was the cheerful guy in my kitchen.

I put my hand on his chest again. "Dominick."

He raised his brow.

"I don't know if this is some foreplay or what, but I need you to be serious right now." I put my hands together, emphasizing my next words. "Gina hooked me up with you as a D appointment. We were only supposed to have sex once."

I chuckled to try to lighten the mood.

Dominick did not.

"Then, we had sex a few more times. But we weren't supposed to be more than a one-time thing. A fling. And that's why I called it off with you."

He studied my face, and after a few seconds, he stripped off his T-shirt. Even in the midst of this strange conversation, I wanted to run my hands over his tattoos and muscles.

"I don't know why you're lying to me again." He pushed his pants and boxers off with one quick shove.

I licked my lips when his dick popped out, all stiff and proud. I looked up at Dominick's face again. "I—"

He grabbed my ponytail and pulled my head back as

he pushed himself against me. His chest was warm against mine, his hard length brushed against my clit, and his mouth was against my ear.

"I said, don't lie to me. Gina sent me a text last week. I know you saw me with her, jumped to conclusions, and called things off with me. Baby, there hasn't been anyone since the moment I met you."

I closed my eyes, hoping if I couldn't see him, I'd feel less like a fool. A fool for misreading the situation and a fool for developing feelings.

"As for the *no condom* thing"—he moved back just enough to shove two fingers inside of me—"that wasn't my goal." He stroked in and out. "In fact, my goal was not to have sex with you at all. But once I saw you, I couldn't help myself." He bit my neck. "Because I've never wanted anyone the way I want you." He pulled his hand away and drove his cock deep inside of me.

I cried out.

"And now that I've had you raw, now that I've had you without anything between us, I'm *never* going back."

"But-but..."

He twisted his hips, and I lost my train of thought.

"But what?"

"But we're not even dating," I managed to pant out as I clawed at his biceps.

He bit my neck again. "Vivian, we are fucking way past dating. You are mine. You are not going anywhere. I'm not going anywhere. You are never getting rid of me."

"But your brother?"

He growled in my ear. "Baby, that had better be the last time you talk about another man while I'm inside you," he said with a pinch to my clit.

I screamed, and my legs shook for a second. "You know what I meant."

"He'll move in here with us. The rest we'll figure out later." He kissed me. "Okay?"

This didn't make sense. None of it made sense. Except that I didn't want him to go. I wanted all the things he'd promised me.

I nodded the best I could since he still had his hand in my hair. "Okay."

"Good girl." He kissed me again. "Now, I'm going to fuck you nice and slow, and when you come, I want you to say my name. Got it?"

"I'll-I'll try."

He finally chuckled. "No trying. You will. You might not realize it, babe, but you went from being silent to the loudest fucking chick I've ever been with."

I gasped, and he laughed as he stopped moving.

Meeting my eyes, he said, "Don't worry. I won't mention another woman again while I'm inside you."

"You'd better fucking not," flew out of my mouth in a tone I hadn't known was possible from me.

"God, I love you." He let go of my hair and wrapped his arms around me. "Now, hang on."

Tilting me backward, he pushed one of my legs over his arm and thoroughly fucked me. Little mewling sounds began to escape from the back of my throat until I was crying out with each thrust from his dick.

As my orgasm drew close, I actually heard myself plead with Dominick. "Please, please, please," I whimpered.

"Shh, it's okay."

"Oh God, I'm going to—"

"I know." He licked his thumb and pushed it between my legs. "Who do you belong to, baby? Say my name," he demanded and strummed my clit.

"*Dominick. Oh God, I love you too,*" I cried out as I exploded and came all over his dick.

EPILOGUE
VIVIAN

"Hey, babe, do you need anything from the store?"

I looked up from my desk to see Dominick standing in the doorway of my new office.

"Nice digs," he said as he stepped inside and nudged the door half-closed.

"Thank you. I'm not a partner yet, but I'm moving up."

My new office was bigger, and my rates had gone up, which meant I had gotten a raise. It was a small change, but I had faith I would reach my goal of making partner someday.

I got up from my chair and walked around to give him a kiss. "What are you doing here?"

He patted the small crossbody pack he was wearing on his chest. "Just about to go and piss some people off."

I laughed. "Subpoena time."

"That's right," he said with a smile. "But I was going to

stop at the store later because Spencer eats too damn much, and I was wondering if you needed anything."

I bit the bottom of my lip to stop the grin that was forming across my face. I failed.

"What?" He raised his eyebrows. "And don't lie to me," he said with a teasing tone.

I plucked his T-shirt. "Nothing. It's just...when I first met you, I would never have thought you would ask me what groceries I needed. Milk and coffee creamer, by the way."

Hauling me into his arms, he said, "And now, you're stuck with me. And speaking of previous punishments..." He slid his hand up my long skirt and cupped my bare ass. "*Mmm*," he groaned into my ear. "I love knowing your cunt is bare for me."

I rubbed my thighs together, wanting him to bring his palm around so he could touch me between my legs. And this was why I wasn't wearing any underwear. Because it turned him on, which turned me on. True to his word, we had sex almost every day, even when I had my period, which was new for me, but I loved that he didn't think I was gross. Something I hadn't realized I'd felt from other guys in the past. And to make this man even sweeter, on my first day, when my cramps were bad, he would bring home ice cream for me and run me a bubble bath, and then he'd send me to bed early without asking to get naked once. He just knew I wasn't up for it.

I'd never thought Dominick was the kind of guy he

was. It showed me that you really couldn't judge a book by its cover.

"I love being bare for you, but I wish there were a way to have you do something similar," I told him.

He laughed. "Babe, I walk around half-hard for you most of the time. No one knows you're not wearing anything under your clothes while I have to hide my goddamn erections throughout the day."

I pursed my lips as I tried not to laugh at him. "Still not quite the same, but I'll take it." I pulled his head down and kissed him.

Just as his tongue swept into my mouth and I was ready to throw a leg over his hip and unbutton his jeans, I heard voices and remembered my door was still ajar.

I stepped back and cleared my throat as I straightened my clothes. "I suppose I should try harder not to get fired so soon after getting a promotion."

Dominick looked at his watch. "I need to get going anyway."

"Me too. I have Women in Law today."

"That's right. I hope it goes well." He started patting down his pants and frowned.

"What's wrong?"

"I can't find my phone. Can you call me?"

"Sure." I found my cell on my desk, pulled up his number, and hit Send.

His pack started vibrating.

I shook my head with a smile and unzipped the front,

so I could pull his phone out. When I saw the screen, I clicked my tongue in disappointment.

"Dominick, you have me in your phone as *V Appointment?*"

He shrugged. "Yeah. And I put me in yours as the opposite."

"But I'm your girlfriend now."

"What do you call me then?" he asked, lifting my hand so he could see my screen. He clicked on Recent Calls and wrinkled his nose. "*Dominick Reyes?*"

"It's your name, obviously," I said.

"But no fun." He took his cell, typed a few things, and turned it around to face me.

"*Baby*," I read out loud.

If I saw anyone else call someone that in their phone, I would roll my eyes, but seeing Dominick call me that made me mushy inside. I was a hypocrite.

"Better?" he asked.

I nodded. "Better."

"Gotta go. Love you." He dropped a peck on my lips.

"I love you too," I said and waved good-bye as he left.

I couldn't stop grinning, and I cleaned up my desk and got my things together for the Women in Law session I had to leave for soon.

There was a knock at my door, and I turned to see Rayne and Delaney standing there.

"Oh my God, I didn't know you two were going to come up to my office," I said.

"You told us about the promotion. We thought we'd

come see the new office in person," Rayne said as I came over and gave her a hug.

"How was your trip with the boyfriend?" I asked. I hadn't seen her before she left town.

She curled her lip. "We broke up."

"I'm sorry. It'd better not be because of your weight or anything. I will hunt him down and—"

"Don't be sorry. And, no, it wasn't because of that. It was almost a worse reason, but I really don't want to talk about it right now."

I nodded in understanding.

"But, hey, we just ran into your man in the hallway. Things are going well, I take it?" Rayne said.

I smiled the kind of smile that only other women understood. "Yes."

"I knew it," Delaney said, and Rayne and I laughed.

"His brother is living with us as of right now, which is kind of different, but Spencer's a great kid."

Rayne smiled. "And to think, you said you didn't like kids."

"Ha. This is different. He's a junior in high school, and he's my brother-in-law. I mean, not really because Dominick and I aren't married, but you get it. And thankfully, he understands that Spencer is going to be the only kid we raise."

When I had brought up the *not wanting kids* situation with Dominick, I really hadn't known which way it would go. Thankfully, he had shrugged and said he wanted what I wanted. He really was the best.

"How's his mom?" Delaney asked.

"She's still in the hospital, but she's awake and sober." I had filled Delaney and Rayne in on the whole situation. "She'll probably be released soon to a nursing home to undergo some physical therapy due to the fire. Not sure when she'll get to go home. Not that she has one yet."

Delaney's expression softened. "I hope everything goes well for Dominick and his brother. Kids like him are why I do what I do."

"Me too. And the court is lucky to have you." I held out my arms. "But this is it. I suppose you two didn't see my previous office, but it was smaller than this one." I had to make that clear because my new one wasn't that big either. "And I'm getting my own assistant. I had to share before, so it's kind of exciting."

"I'm happy for you, Vivian," Rayne said.

"I am too," Delaney said.

"Thank you both."

Delaney looked at her phone. "I suppose we should go."

"Oh, yes. We should."

I grabbed my purse, and the three of us headed for the elevator. When we were almost there, Preston St. James came around the corner, and he and Delaney both froze.

"Delaney," he said, his face still in shock.

Her gaze dipped to the open collar of his white shirt. Preston was muscular and tan, and I could see why my friend had fallen for him.

She swallowed hard before hiking her purse up onto her shoulder and straightening her spine. "Hey, Pres."

"What are you doing here?" he asked.

"I came to see Vivian's new office."

When Delaney turned in the direction of where we'd just come from, Preston's eyes darted down to her ass, and fire flared in his eyes.

I scooted closer to Rayne and silently grabbed her arm. She nodded subtly.

She'd noticed it too.

Preston licked the corner of his mouth, but he seemed to realize where he was and who was in his presence, and he schooled his face just as Delaney turned back to him.

Rayne and I immediately looked away, so he wouldn't catch us watching him, but I should've been more careful because my eyes landed right on his crotch.

Holy shit. Preston St. James had a huge hard-on for his ex-wife.

I darted my eyes away again. I had never felt more awkward at my place of employment as I did at this moment.

Mercifully, Rayne came to the rescue. "Sorry to break this up, but we need to leave." She stuck out her hand. "I'm Rayne Thompson."

Preston shook it. "Preston St. James."

Delaney cleared her throat. Her posture was stiff. Almost as if she was trying to keep herself from moving. "Rayne is right. We need to go. We have an appointment for Women in Law."

"I heard that's going well," he said.

Delaney looked at me. I hoped she wasn't upset I had talked about our project. He was my superior and the one who had assigned it to me.

"Yes, it is."

Preston nodded. "Good. That's good to hear." He smiled politely at Rayne and me. "I'll leave you to it then." He stepped around us and disappeared down the hallway.

The three of us walked to the elevator without another word, but once the doors closed, Delaney collapsed against the wall.

"Delaney, I'm sorry to say this," Rayne said, "but your ex-husband is *fine*." She waved her hand against her face. "And the sparks coming off the two of you? *Whew*. Why the hell did you get a divorce?"

"You know earlier, when you said you didn't want to talk about it?" Delaney asked.

Rayne nodded.

"That's me now."

"Got it."

"I didn't know seeing him was going to be so awkward."

"But you must see each other all the time?" I said. Instantly, I held up my hand. "Sorry. You said you didn't want to talk about it."

"Paxton's nanny brings him back and forth between the two of us. And before that, it was my ex-mother-in-law." Delaney curled her lip at the mention of Preston's mother. "I hadn't seen him in months."

The elevator doors opened, and she pushed herself forward.

"Looks like Delaney and I both have exes we don't want to talk about," Rayne said with a chuckle as we followed Delaney out.

"Yeah," I agreed. "Maybe someday, you'll both tell your stories." I hoped so anyway.

"Maybe," Rayne said. "But today is definitely not that day."

TURN THE PAGE FOR A SAMPLE OF
THE C AGREEMENT

THE C AGREEMENT
CADE

My eyes fell to Rayne's plump lip as she chewed on it. I could almost see the wheels turning behind her brown eyes, and I couldn't help but smile.

"What's your idea?" I asked. I couldn't wait to see what she was concocting in her cute head.

Beau dangling our restaurant in front of me was definitely the most tempting thing he could have offered for me to agree to this bet of his. The only problem was, I had no desire to settle down with anyone, and the thought of picking one woman to screw for a month almost made my dick shrivel up. Almost. The reason I had multiple regulars was because I liked to fuck. A lot. I didn't want anyone to get too attached to me, which was why I spread repeat visits out. And sleeping with someone regularly for thirty-one days might give them the wrong idea. But the alternative sounded worse. Going a whole month with zero sex sounded like torture.

So, if Rayne had an idea of how I could win this bet without getting tied down with someone, I was all ears.

She looked down at herself, then back up to me. "Never mind," she said with a chuckle. "It was a silly thought."

She started to face forward again, but I stopped her with a hand on her knee.

"I doubt that." I rubbed my thumb over her smooth skin. "Tell me. Let me decide if it's silly."

She arched her neck and looked around before relaxing back in her seat. "If I tell you this, it stays between the two of us, okay?"

My eyebrows flew up. While I considered Rayne a friend, she was my best friend's little sister first, and I didn't think we'd ever had a secret that we kept from Beau. Or Em for that matter.

"It doesn't concern my brother or Em, but it is embarrassing, which is why I don't want anyone to know," she added when I didn't answer her.

I nodded. "Your secret is safe with me."

Rayne opened her mouth, paused, grabbed her margarita, and downed the rest.

I chuckled. "Liquid courage?"

"Yeah, something like that."

Rubbing my thumb on her knee, I said, "Take your time."

"Can't. Beau and Em will be back soon, and I absolutely do *not* want my brother to hear this." She sucked in a big breath and then exhaled.

"Rayne, it can't be that—"

"I suck in bed," she blurted out.

What?

"What?"

"Really? You're going to make me say it again?"

I shook my head. I'd heard her the first time. "I guess I don't understand."

Breaking eye contact, she muttered, "Brett and I broke up because he said that he would rather fuck a dead fish than me." Her cheeks turned bright red.

My body was also heating up, but for an entirely different reason. "*What the fuck?*"

Rayne jumped as her eyes flew back to mine. "Shh...I don't need anyone to know about this. I haven't even told any of my friends." Dropping her head in her hands, she said, "It's so humiliating."

I tugged on her wrists. "No, it's not."

She shot me a *don't be ridiculous* look. "If I were eighteen, sure, but I'm almost thirty. I should know what I'm doing in bed."

Not if she'd had lousy-ass lovers.

But saying that out loud wasn't going to lessen her embarrassment, so I just told her the truth. "What an asshole."

"Yes. But also, no."

"There is no *no* about it."

She lifted a shoulder. "If he hadn't told me, then I wouldn't have known I needed to fix it."

I ground my teeth together. One person's opinion didn't make it fact.

"But that's where my idea comes in."

"What idea?"

She chuckled, and I was happy to see something other than despair on her face.

"My idea. For the bet."

My brow furrowed. "What does one have to do with the other?"

Oh shit.

Don't say it.

Please don't say—

"I'll have sex with you for the month—no strings attached—and in turn, you can help me become a better lover."

She said it.

She bit her lip again when I didn't say anything. "What do you think? You'll get your restaurant, and I'll get better in bed."

"No."

RAYNE

I frowned. "No? What do you mean, no?"

I thought it seemed like the perfect plan, but then he eyed me up and down, assessing me.

And it clicked.

"I get it." I felt the heat rise to my cheeks once again.

How many times did I have to be mortified in one night? Make that, in the last ten minutes.

He snorted. "You do?"

"Yeah." And because I was a little pissed off that he wouldn't even consider my idea, I decided to put him on the spot. It was only fair that he felt awkward too. "You're not into fat chicks."

I had done a lot of work on myself and my body, and I'd come to find parts of myself that were attractive. But I sometimes forgot that everyone else in my life still lived by societal standards, and looking back, I had never seen Cade with a fat woman before. Thicker women? Sure. Voluptuous women? Definitely. Fat? No.

He scowled and slowly turned toward me. "What the fuck did you say?" he growled through clenched teeth.

Whoa.

I swallowed. I didn't see him mad a lot, and I didn't know what to do. "Uh..." My eyes darted around before coming back to him. "You're not attracted to me." I shrugged, trying to show him it was okay even if I felt like a fool for offering myself up for sex. "It's not a big deal."

I slumped back in my seat, wishing Beau and Em would come back so this night could end. I wanted to pay my bill and get out of there. It looked like I was the only one who was going to feel any sort of embarrassment tonight because Cade was definitely not.

"Just please don't say anything to anyone," I whispered.

I suddenly pictured Cade telling his friends—minus my brother—about my proposition and them all laughing at the fat chick for even thinking she had a chance.

I didn't cry or feel sorry for myself a lot, but I could feel the unwelcome burning in the backs of my eyes. Just what I needed to complete my night.

"Get out," I demanded with a lift of my chin.

Cade was still staring at me, so I knew he'd heard me.

"Rayne." His jaw was hard, and he had the audacity to look mad at me.

I grabbed my purse. "Get. Out." I wished I were smaller, so I could climb over him to get out of the booth, but even attempting it would just remind us both why he had turned me down.

"I'm not moving until we talk."

Is he serious? I had lived twenty-nine years, having guys explain to me that they saw me as just a friend. Or that I had a pretty face, but they didn't like me that way. He didn't need to feed me all his bullshit. I'd been hearing it my whole life.

I got in his face until we were nose to nose. "Get the fuck out of my way before I scream."

His eyes narrowed, but surprisingly, he turned away and got out of the booth.

I scrambled out before he could change his mind. "Tell my brother I'll send him some money for dinner," I said over my shoulder and bolted out of the restaurant.

I hoped Cade lost the fucking bet.

ABOUT THE AUTHOR

R.L. Kenderson is two best friends writing under one name.

Renae has always loved reading, and in third grade, she wrote her first poem where she learned she might have a knack for this writing thing. Lara remembers sneaking her grandmother's Harlequin novels when she was probably too young to be reading them, and since then, she knew she wanted to write her own.

When they met in college, they bonded over their love of reading and the TV show *Charmed*. What really spiced up their friendship was when Lara introduced Renae to romance novels. When they discovered their first vampire romance, they knew there would always be a special place in their hearts for paranormal romance. After being unable to find certain storylines and characteristics they wanted to read about in the hundreds of books they consumed, they decided to write their own.

One lives in the Minneapolis-St. Paul area and the other in the Kansas City area where they both work in the medical field during the day and a sexy author by night. They communicate through phone, email, and whole lot of messaging.

You can find them at http://www.rlkenderson.com, Facebook, Instagram, TikTok, and Goodreads. Join their reader group! Or you can email them at rlkenderson@rlkenderson.com, or sign up for their newsletter. They always love hearing from their readers.